59372089183035   FTBC

WITHD~

WORN, SOILED, OBSOL

D0053632

THE SKELETON TREE

ALSO BY IAIN LAWRENCE

The Giant-Slayer

The Séance

Gemini Summer

B for Buster

The Lightkeeper's Daughter

Lord of the Nutcracker Men

Ghost Boy

THE CURSE OF THE JOLLY STONE TRILOGY

The Convicts

The Cannibals

The Castaways

THE HIGH SEAS TRILOGY

The Wreckers

The Smugglers

The Buccaneers

THE SKELETON TREE

IAIN LAWRENCE

DELACORTE PRESS

This is a work of fiction. Names, characters, places, and incidents either are the product of the author's imagination or are used fictitiously. Any resemblance to actual persons, living or dead, events, or locales is entirely coincidental.

Text copyright © 2016 by Iain Lawrence
Jacket art copyright © 2016 by Daniel Burgess

All rights reserved. Published in the United States by Delacorte Press, an imprint of Random House Children's Books, a division of Penguin Random House LLC, New York.

Delacorte Press is a registered trademark and the colophon is a trademark of Penguin Random House LLC.

Visit us on the Web! randomhousekids.com

Educators and librarians, for a variety of teaching tools, visit us at RHTeachersLibrarians.com

Library of Congress Cataloging-in-Publication Data
Lawrence, Iain
The skeleton tree / by Iain Lawrence. — First edition.
pages cm
Summary: "Chris and Frank's sailing vessel sinks and they are stranded alone in the wilds of Alaska. They don't like each other at all, but to survive they must build a relationship"—Provided by publisher.
ISBN 978-0-385-73378-6 (hardback) — ISBN 978-0-385-90395-0 (glb) — ISBN 978-0-307-97489-1 (ebook)
[1. Survival—Fiction. 2. Wilderness areas—Fiction. 3. Brothers—Fiction. 4. Alaska—Fiction.] I. Title.
PZ7.L43545Sk 2016
[Fic]—dc23
2015011779

The text of this book is set in 11.25-point Village.
Jacket design by Kate Gartner
Interior design by Heather Kelly

Printed in the United States of America
10 9 8 7 6 5 4 3 2 1
First Edition

Random House Children's Books supports the First Amendment and celebrates the right to read.

For Françoise

With happy memories

1

The Last Morning

When I wake in the night, I'm afraid.

I lie staring through blackness, listening for every sound from the forest. I can't see the ceiling or the walls of the cabin. I can't see Frank, and for a moment I'm sure that he's gone. But then, through the dark, comes the fluttery sound of his breathing, and I feel safe to know that he's near.

I used to be scared all the time, and nights were the worst. When the sun went down, I felt like screaming. I'm not the same anymore. I've learned many things about the forest and the sea, and many things about myself. But when I wake in the dark, I'm afraid.

Out in the forest, something is waiting. It's staying as still and silent as I am, both of us listening.

Is it the grizzly bear? I can imagine it standing huge

and shaggy right beside the cabin, just the thickness of the wall away. But it might be a wolf. We've heard them singing, every night a little closer. It could be a man. Or it could even be a skeleton. I've heard them stirring in their coffins. These are things from my nightmares, and they loom in my mind in a terrifying cycle.

I always think of the worst things first. But it's probably a squirrel out there. Or a deer that will flee in a moment, crashing through the forest in leaps and bounds. I hope it's my night-black raven, come home at last from his wandering. But I'm afraid to call out. Through the cabin wall, through the stillness of the night, we must feel each other waiting. We're just two creatures in the darkness.

I don't know how much time passes before the window begins to brighten. Maybe it only *feels* like hours. But long before the sun will rise, the square of plastic starts to shine with a gray light. Shadows of trees appear like etches on a slate. Through the cracks of the cabin walls shine little gleams of gold.

With morning, my fears vanish. And so does that thing in the forest. There's no burst of noise, no thudding feet. I don't hear it leave, but I know it's gone. I have lived long enough in the wilderness that I sense things like that.

Quickly now, the darkness of the cabin dissolves into shadows, and the shadows change as they harden. Mushrooms sprout from the floor and become the stones of the fire circle. A skinny-legged beast morphs into our driftwood table. Monstrous men stand in the corner, then slip into the plastic capes that hang from their pegs.

I see the stack of firewood, the bottles of water, the shoes piled high beneath the table. I guess I went a bit stupid with shoes. I see all the things I've carried from the beach, the stuff Frank calls junk. But to me it's important because it came across the sea from Japan. I like to wonder about those things, to invent their stories.

Near the floor where Frank is sleeping, pale scratches in the wall mark the days that have passed. They're squashed together, blurred into one long smudge just like the days themselves: thirty, forty, fifty of them, and all the same.

Then I remember that this day is different. Today is the day we'll be saved.

It's still early, at least an hour till dawn. But I can't wait that long. I have to go down to the skeleton tree.

I roll out of bed and crouch over Frank. Not long ago I would have been afraid to wake him like this. He would have gotten very angry very fast. But this morning I think he won't mind. I shake him by the shoulder, shouting his name, and his hands swing up to fight me. He springs away with a cry, thumping his back against the cabin wall. His eyes are huge and startled, and when he sees me, he groans. "What's the matter with you?" he asks. "Are you crazy?"

"Today's the day," I tell him.

"Stop shouting," he grumbles.

I can't understand why he isn't excited. Frank's only three years older than me, not even sixteen. But sometimes he seems almost grown up. He scratches his matted hair and squints at the window. "It's not even morning, Chris."

"But they might be landing right now," I tell him. "Don't you want to see that?"

He coughs and shakes his head. "You go ahead. I want to sleep some more. But start the fire first; I'm cold."

Even a month ago it would have made me angry to be told what to do. But now I know it's just Frank's way. I squat by the circle of stones and scrape at the ashes with a small stick. The coals underneath are still warm and glimmering. In their glow I see my breath, a little red cloud like dragon's fire. I arrange a few twigs and a sprig of dry moss, and as I lean forward to blow on the embers, smoke rises into my eyes, making me squint. But flames come quickly. I'm an expert now at starting fires, maybe better than Frank.

I add more wood. The smoke grows thick and ropy, swirling up to the ceiling and out through the hole. I can imagine pictures forming in front of me, images that whirl apart and form again.

My uncle Jack told me once that if you look too long at a fire it will steal your thoughts away. He was right.

2

The Daredevil

My mother tried to warn me about Uncle Jack. "He's a daredevil," she said. "He can't be happy unless he's facing danger."

But I loved my uncle. He raced motorcycles; he jumped out of airplanes; he fought forest fires for a living. My father was an accountant who drove a brown minivan and worked in an office. It was no wonder that Uncle Jack was my hero when I was small.

He went away on long adventures, sometimes for months at a time. When my father died and Uncle Jack turned up for the funeral, I hardly recognized him. He stayed only three days, then vanished again. He bought a boat and set off to sail around the world.

It was almost exactly a year later when he came back

into my life. My mother answered the phone and there he was, talking from the dock in Kodiak, Alaska.

They had a long conversation that she made sure I couldn't hear. She turned her back and whispered strange things in a strange voice, all beginning, "Oh, Jack."

"Oh, Jack, do you think that's a good idea?"

"Oh, Jack, Christopher doesn't know about any of that."

"Oh, Jack, I'm just not sure it's the right thing for him now."

When she hung up the phone she was red and flustered.

"What don't I know about, Mom?" I asked.

She stared at me. "Well, sailing," she said. "For starters. Jack wants you to fly up to Kodiak and sail home on the boat."

I wasn't sure what to say, or even what I felt. I hardly knew my uncle anymore, and I had never been on a sailboat.

"You realize you'd have to miss nearly a month of school," said Mom, and suddenly sailing with Uncle Jack seemed like a great idea. I begged her to let me go.

"It might be a learning opportunity," I told her.

"No doubt," said Mom, with a little snort. "I'm just not sure I want you learning what Jack would teach you."

She stood at the bookshelves, where a jumble of

pictures showed my father as a boy. In one he was peering up through the poles of a lean-to. In another he was holding a fishing rod and a huge salmon. But my mother picked up the only one of my dad and Uncle Jack together. They looked almost like opposites, one short and dark, the other tall and fair, one thin and one muscled. They sat on the back of a horse that had no saddle, Uncle Jack in front, my father behind him, peering around his shoulder. They wore nothing but shorts, and little war bonnets made of cardboard, with painted feathers that stuck straight up. They were suntanned and smiling, and my father looked really happy in a way that I could sort of remember.

"Oh, I don't know what's best," said Mom. "Maybe a bit of adventure is what you need right now. But you have to be careful of men who love danger. Even Jack."

She dusted the picture with her sleeve, then put it back in its place and sighed. "All right, you can go," she said. "I just hope I won't live to regret it."

Less than a week later I was on an airplane flying up the coast. Around my neck hung a sign that said *Unaccompanied Minor*. It was a month after my twelfth birthday, but the flight attendants—like almost everyone else—thought I was more like nine or ten. They made a big fuss over me because I was a little kid traveling by myself. They talked in that embarrassing way that grown-ups use for children, with phony voices and phony smiles.

All the way north I stared through the window at endless rows of mountains. Although it was nearly the middle of August, vast fields of snow gleamed in the sunshine. I imagined I could see a thousand square miles at once, but not a single house, not a road, not a sign of people anywhere.

I pictured the plane making an emergency landing on a glacier, and me crawling from the wreckage to find that I was the only survivor. I could see myself standing on one of those mountaintops, screaming for help, with no one to hear me.

We arrived in Kodiak five hours late, after the sun had set. A flight attendant took my hand and walked me through the terminal as though I was a little boy. Uncle Jack laughed when he saw me. He tore off the sign and flung it like a Frisbee toward a garbage can. "You don't need *that* nonsense anymore," he said.

We took a taxi to the dock, where Uncle Jack had parked his boat. It was called *Puff*, and it looked too small to have gone all the way around the world. Tiny portholes glowed with yellow light from the cabin. When Uncle Jack pushed open the hatch and led me down a steep ladder, I was surprised to see a kid sprawled along a bench.

He was older than me by two or three years. His arms were long and tanned, and his black hair hung over his eyes. Uncle Jack put his hands on my shoulders and told the kid, "Say hello to Chrissy."

I wished he hadn't used that dorky name from my childhood. By the little flicker that came into the kid's eyes I knew he'd tease me about it later.

The boy heaved himself up from the table. Thinking he meant to shake hands, I reached shyly toward him. But he only tossed his head to flick the hair from his eyes and told Uncle Jack, "I'm going to bed."

"Don't you want to stay up for a while?" asked Uncle Jack. "Have a gam, as the whalers used to say?"

"No," said the kid. He pushed past me and slouched away.

"Hey, Frank, come on," said Uncle Jack, disappointed. But the kid kept going, through a narrow door at the front of the boat.

We watched him go. Then Uncle Jack sort of laughed and said, "That's Franklin."

Franklin? I nearly laughed. It was an old-fashioned name that didn't suit the kid at all. The only Franklin I'd ever known was my grandfather, a human prune named after President Roosevelt.

"Who *is* he?" I asked.

"Well, that's a long story," said Uncle Jack. "And it's a little late tonight. So let's wait till tomorrow, till we're under way, and you can both hear it."

"He's coming with us?" I asked.

Uncle Jack started nodding, then kept going like a bobblehead doll. "Yeah. I guess he is."

We spent the night at the dock. At first I felt awkward

being around Uncle Jack again. But he was very kind. He showed me all the things he'd collected on his voyage, then talked about my dad. He told funny stories' I'd never heard before, and he said how much he missed my dad, and that he could only imagine how hard it was for me.

"Your father loved you more than he loved the whole world," said Uncle Jack. "I hope you know that."

I slept on a narrow bed that Uncle Jack called his sea berth. And I woke early, to hear seagulls crying outside. But Franklin didn't get out of bed until Uncle Jack went in three times to wake him. Then he dragged himself around without saying a word. He kept flicking his hair out of his eyes, as though hair flicking was his favorite hobby. He never smiled or anything. He was the sort of kid who looked as though he was always making fun of people inside his head.

He sat down at the table and took out an iPod. Quick as a snake, Uncle Jack snatched it from his hands.

"Give that back!" cried the kid.

Uncle Jack shook his head. "There's no place at sea for gadgets. Believe me, you'll find plenty to keep you interested." He asked if we had other things, and took them all away. He even took the kid's wristwatch because it had a game built into it. "Yours too, Chrissy," he said, waggling his fingers.

"But it's just a watch. See?" I turned my wrist to show him the dial. "It was a present from my dad."

"Yeah, okay," he said. Everything else went into a box that he locked in a drawer. "Now for the tour. Because Frank slept in, we'll have to hurry."

In one quick sweep, Uncle Jack led us through the boat. He showed us how to start the engine, where to find the flares, how to work the little VHF radio if we had to call for help, and he did it all in just a minute or two. Then we trooped up the ladder and out to the deck.

"I'll get us shipshape," said Uncle Jack. "You boys go forward and haul the dinghy aboard."

"Tell *him* to do it," said the kid.

"I'm telling you both to do it."

The dinghy was a little red boat sitting on the dock. Made of plywood, blunt at both ends, it looked small and worn-out. Lashed to the seats was a pair of stubby oars and a plastic scoop tied to a bit of old string. Frank took one end and I took the other. But he pulled too hard and yanked the boat right out of my hands. Flakes of red paint scattered across the planks as it fell on the dock.

Uncle Jack looked up. "Be careful there, Chris," he said. "That's our lifeboat."

"Our *lifeboat*?" I asked.

"It's all you need," said Uncle Jack. "If you know what you're doing."

There was no wind that morning, so he used the diesel engine, and we headed out to sea. Over big, smooth

11

waves we soared like a slow roller coaster, the three of us sitting at the back, in the place that Uncle Jack called the cockpit. The big steering wheel was there, and so many ropes lying all over the place that I felt as though I was sitting in a bowl of spaghetti. The kid stuffed his hands in his pockets, flicked away his hair for the nine thousandth time, and stared right past us.

"We'll get clear of the coast, then put up the sails and have our little talk," said Uncle Jack, shouting above the sound of the engine. "If you start feeling queasy, let me know. I can give you pills that'll take care of that."

I was already feeling queasy, but I didn't want to say so. Frank looked fine, and I was determined not to be the only one to get sick. The boat lifted on the waves and slid down their backs, and the smell of exhaust floated around us. I felt my breakfast slosh inside my stomach.

The land faded behind us. Uncle Jack kept pointing out interesting things, but I was too woozy to turn my head. I just slumped there and watched garbage floating past. Plastic bottles, metal barrels, fishing floats, they all bobbed dizzily on the waves. Uncle Jack said it was debris from a tsunami that had hit Japan more than two years earlier. "This is nothing," he told us. "There's a whole floating island of garbage out there. I kid you not. I saw it in front of me one morning and thought I was going to run aground." He steered the boat with one hand, lounging in the sun. "I'll spare you the details, but I saw things that don't bear thinking about."

"Really? Like what?" Frank sat up like a squirrel, his eyes bright. "Things like bodies?"

"You don't want to know," said Uncle Jack, which made me think they must have been terrible things. "The point is, it's all going to wash up on the shore one day. In some places, it's washing up already."

Around noon, I started thinking I might throw up. I thought no one could tell, but Frank cried in a delighted voice, "Look at him! He's turning green."

"I think we need something to eat," said Uncle Jack. He went down to the cabin and clattered through draw-ers. When he brought up the lunch, so did I. The smell of Spam and ketchup made my stomach twist, and in one hot rush everything spewed out through my nose and mouth.

"Oh, gross!" said Frank.

Uncle Jack made me lie down in the cabin. He gave me a big blue pill to make me sleep. Then he gave me another just to make sure. Still in my boots and jacket, zipped into my sleeping bag, I lay in a bed that heaved and tossed, and I dreamed of those things that didn't bear thinking about.

It seemed whole days went by. Confused by the blue pills, I couldn't tell what was real and what was not. I was sure that my father brought me a glass of water, and that a seagull flew into the cabin and told me a story. I was aware at one point that the engine had stopped. Through the open hatch, I could see the sail full of wind, glaring white in the sun as *Puff* rushed along.

I dreamed terrible dreams. Zombies chased me across an island made of garbage. One of them caught me and held me down; he started to rip my arms off, and I woke wrestling with Uncle Jack. "Chrissy, it's all right," he said. He'd brought water and soup, but I wasn't hungry. He talked in a voice that was loud and distorted, and he stared at me with a worried look as I fell again into woozy nightmares.

The sea gurgled past; the waves whooshed and burst. There was sunlight and darkness, and all I wanted was to get off the boat and onto solid land. Then something jolted me out of my sleep. I heard a shout, a bang, and *Puff* came to a shuddering stop. The floorboards burst from their places as the sea came roaring through the hull.

The blue pills made everything seem unreal. But ice-cold water rose over my bed. And I knew the boat was sinking.

The Lifeboat

I am aware that Frank has been talking to me. He brings this to my attention by kicking me in the butt. He doesn't have to get up from his bed to do it. He just swings his leg and boots me.

"Hey!" he shouts. "Are you all right?"

Embers crackle in the fire. Flames leap through the smoke, casting their strange pictures. I nod to tell Frank I'm all right. "I was just thinking."

"Well, go think outside," he says. "You're creeping me out."

I take a plastic bucket and fill it quickly with the things I'll need: a plastic cape and my tattered poncho; the paperback book with its ragged pages; a bottle of water and half of our last piece of fish. When I open the door, the trees tower above me, reaching down with shaggy branches. From the sea comes the soft bursting of the waves, as though the forest is breathing.

The trail is a dark tunnel through the salal bushes. Anything could be hiding in there, and six weeks ago I would not have dared to go alone. Even now, with the bear and the wolves in my mind, I wish I had waited for Frank. But I know every twist and bend. I've learned my way through *all* the things that scare me. I just duck my head and run.

Branches snatch at my bucket. Roots try hard to trip me, but I keep going, and as soon as I reach the clearing I see the skeleton tree. It stands alone on the grass-covered rocks, its branches twisting across the sky. The black shapes of the coffins rest in its gnarled arms, and I don't look up as I dash underneath them, straight to the rocky shore where the wooden saint looks blindly out to sea.

I feel terrible disappointment to find the ocean black and empty. There's no Coast Guard ship, no helicopter. There's nothing but my memories.

It was somewhere out there on the waves that heave and roll, that I last saw Uncle Jack.

• • •

I screamed his name as the sea came gushing into the cabin. But no one came running down to save me.

In the open hatch floated puffy clouds bright with

sunshine. The steering wheel gleamed, and the big sail thrashed back and forth as ropes stretched and shuddered. I felt a sudden dread that Uncle Jack had taken the kid and gone away, that I was abandoned on a sinking boat.

I squirmed in my sleeping bag. I rolled myself off the bed and sank into ice-cold water that made me gasp. *Puff* wallowed, and I fell, first against the counter and then against the stove before I fled up the ladder to the cockpit. There was no land in sight.

I turned around and looked toward the bow, and there was Uncle Jack—and Frank as well—trying to free the little red dinghy that really had become our lifeboat.

Puff's bow plunged into the sea, then soared up again with water streaming in silvery sheets. Frank was on his knees, clinging to the rigging as spray flew over him. Uncle Jack slashed at the ropes with a knife, and the waves were enormous.

Sunlight flashed on the blade. Then the little boat suddenly sprang from its place. Snatched by a wave, it was pulled right over the lifelines, dragged away by the sea until it snubbed up at the end of its tether.

"Get in!" shouted Uncle Jack. But Frank didn't move.

Uncle Jack had to pry the kid's fingers from the rigging. He picked him up and balanced on the pitching deck, his feet far apart. He looked big and heroic with the sea raging behind him. When the dinghy shot up on a wave, he dropped the kid inside it. Then he turned around and made his way toward me, reaching for handholds as the sea swept over the deck.

He clambered into the cockpit. "Did you bring the radio?" he asked.

"No," I said. The dinghy soared high above us on a passing wave, then dropped below the railing. The kid lay inside it, unmoving.

"The flares?" said Uncle Jack. "The life jackets?"

I shook my head. I could hardly think.

"Wait here."

He plunged down the ladder, into the cabin. The water was chest-high and rising fast. Everything that could float was swirling around and around.

"Uncle Jack, come back!" I shouted.

He looked right at me for a moment. "Get in the lifeboat, Chrissy," he said. Then he moved farther into the cabin, pushing his way through a floating mass of cushions and floorboards and blankets.

The deck that had once seemed so high was now level with the sea. Only the low roof of the cabin stood above the water, and every wave surged through the cockpit.

"Uncle Jack!" I cried.

It looked as though a river was flowing through the hatch and into the cabin. I saw Uncle Jack take the VHF radio from its place, but the water pushed against him and he couldn't get back to the cockpit.

"Here!" he shouted. "Catch." He tossed the radio up toward me.

I tried to grab it. For a moment I had it in my hands. But it fell away. I lunged to grab it again, and nearly tumbled through the hatch myself. I grabbed on to its edges as the radio vanished into the swirls of black water, and I saw Uncle Jack looking up at me. I saw fear and sorrow in his expression—and something else as well. I had let him down.

The sea gushed through the hatch. It rose right over Uncle Jack, sucking him into the darkness. Then enormous bubbles burst through the hatch, and the deck slipped away from my feet, and I was floating in the sea.

The top of the cabin vanished. The lifelines dipped into the water. When the little red dinghy swirled over them, I tumbled inside it. The kid was sitting upright now, but he didn't say a word and he stared straight ahead. His hands clutched like talons to the sides of the boat.

The sea was full of ropes and sails, of things that had burst loose from the cabin. I saw boxes of crackers, a loaf of bread, some of Uncle Jack's souvenirs. Then, afraid *Puff* would drag us down, I struggled with the rope that held us. There was a knot too tight to untie, and I went at it with my hands, then with my teeth. The lifeboat tipped up on one end. The bow went under. I could see *Puff* down below, a shadowy thing far under the surface. Then, at last, with a snap, the rope tore away, and the lifeboat slapped flat on the water. We began to drift with the wind, lurching over the waves.

By then, *Puff* was gone. There was nothing but that terrible sea all around us. In the little red boat we skidded and whirled down the waves. I screamed until my throat was sore.

"Uncle Jack!"

"Uncle Jack!"

But there was no echo on the sea. And of course nobody answered.

The blue pills had worn off, but everything still seemed dreamily unreal as we floated in that little red boat. As it reeled over the waves, Frank sat without moving. He didn't even shift his weight to keep us level. His jacket zipped up to his chin, his hands clamped to the sides of the boat, he looked right at me without seeing me.

At the other end I leaned forward or sideways or backward to keep us level. But water still slopped over the sides and soon filled the boat to our ankles.

The plastic scoop had tangled around the oars. I snapped it from its string and started bailing. I looked at my watch many times before I realized it had stopped. Seeing the hands frozen in place made me feel angry and hopeless. I leaned back my head and shouted at the sea and the sky.

At sunset, the wind fell. The waves began to flatten, and there was no danger then of sinking. But I felt more frightened than ever as I watched the sky turn red. In that tiny boat far from land, I began to wonder what Uncle Jack had really seen. What if all the people who had been swept to sea were floating along around us?

In every way, I was adrift in the dark. I didn't know where I was going or what I would find; I just wished I was home with my mother. I pictured her standing at the big front window, looking out at the same darkness, thinking of me just as I was thinking of her. But she would have no idea that I was lost on the ocean. She would imagine me sailing happily with Uncle Jack.

Darkness settled. Then stars choked the sky—more stars than I had ever seen. Across them drifted satellites, flying along with a silent, steady purpose that made me feel horribly lonesome.

Frank sat as rigid as ever, rising up against the stars when the boat lifted on the waves. Shivering with cold, I tightened my sodden jacket and rubbed my arms to keep warm.

At dawn I saw clouds in the distance. Then, under the clouds I saw land, a line of jagged mountains with snow-covered tops. Currents and winds were pushing us in that direction, but so slowly that I thought we might never reach shore. Frank's fingers were white and wrinkled, like drowned worms hooked over the edge of the boat. His teeth ticked as they chattered, and little tremors ran through him, twitching around his eyes. I was terribly afraid he would die. I worried about what would happen if he did. I couldn't sit with a dead boy, but how could I roll him out of the boat and watch him sink into the water's blue darkness?

I pried out the oars and began to row. For hours and hours I rowed that boat. My hands grew blisters, and the salt water that trickled down the oars made them burn. The sides of the boat warped in and out, until little bubbles started streaming up through the corners. Water oozed through the bottom. Rowing the boat would destroy it, but I had no choice.

At the end of the day the mountains looked huge. The land appeared wild and empty, and when the sun went down there was not a single light along that huge shore, not a sign of people anywhere. Then the wind began to rise again, and the waves grew taller, and sometime before dawn I heard the rumbling sound of surf.

I raised my head to look around. In the pale moonlight, ghostly plumes of spray appeared. The surf grew louder, and I saw streaks of foam shredded from the crests of enormous waves. The boat rushed like a sled through the darkness. I tore off my jacket, hoping I could row harder without it, and tried to drive the little boat away from land. But we were swept in among the breakers, and one hammered down on us.

The oars flew away as I tumbled into the sea. Gasping from the cold, I struggled to the surface. My flailing hands clutched on to the boat. Now upside down, it arched out of the sea like a turtle, and I gripped its little spine and held myself there.

Ten feet away, in the gray foam of the breakers, Frank floated facedown. His black hair shone, flat and smooth. His jacket puffed out around his back, swollen with air and holding his arms splayed across the water. I could hold on to the boat and ride it to shore, or I could let go of my last hope and try to save Frank. But I barely thought about it. I pushed away from the boat and grabbed Frank. I held on to his jacket, on to his collar, on to his arms while a tumbling wave tried to tear us apart.

He snapped awake.

His head shook like a dog's, flinging water from his hair. His eyes grew impossibly big. And then, with both hands, he clutched onto me, pinning my arms to my sides.

I couldn't swim; I couldn't even keep us afloat. But the more I struggled to get away, the more Frank fought to hold me. We both sank underwater, and the next wave drove us deeper. It rolled us over and over in a frozen darkness. It scraped us across the rocks on the bottom, then spun us up to the surface. I gasped as the surf thundered around us, and I kept my arm around Frank, lifting his head out of the water.

We were just tiny things in that surf, pushed here and there, pummeled and punched. The waves whirled us along, but every one swept us closer to land, and the seventh—or the eighth or the ninth—slammed us down on a stony beach. With a rumble and clatter it drained away and left us stranded.

I heard the boom of the next wave smashing. It pushed us higher up the beach, then tried to pull us back as it drained away in a gurgling rush through the stones. I grabbed a rock and held on.

Wave after wave reached up to get us. They pulled away my boots, one after the other. They pulled Frank out of my arms and dragged him down the beach. On his back he slithered, spread-eagled, over the moonlit stones, screaming at me to save him. I grabbed his leg and crawled up the beach like a crab, scuttling a few feet at a time.

My hands were bleeding. My knee throbbed. But I kept moving up from the sea, and Frank crawled along behind me like some terrible creature slithering from the depths. At the top of the beach we found a cliff, and we sat with our backs against it.

I couldn't believe how I'd tumbled so quickly from an ordinary life into my very worst nightmare. I was stranded in the wilderness with a kid who seemed barely alive, and I had no idea who he was.

At dawn I looked out on a dreadful world. Waves

thundered into the cove and hurled themselves at the stones below us.

A line of kelp and seaweed lay bundled like rope along the base of the cliff. But there was not a stick of driftwood, and that puzzled me for a moment. Then I realized what it meant. At high tide, the beach would disappear. The cove would fill like a huge bucket, and we would drown like mice inside it.

I shoved Frank's shoulder. "Get up," I told him.

He groaned. He pushed my hand away. But he lifted his head and looked around, then dragged himself to the cliff. He pressed a hand against the rock where a trickle of water made it black and shiny.

In a very little while, his palm began to fill. He slurped up the water and filled it again, and beside him I did the same thing. Together, we drank water from the stone. When he'd had enough, Frank turned to the seaweed and pulled out a handful of leaves. They looked like lettuce gone bad in a crisper, but Frank shook off the pebbles and twigs, the tiny shells, and stuffed the seaweed into his mouth. The sound of his chewing made my stomach gurgle. I had eaten nothing since my night at the dock in *Puff.*

"How do you know that's safe?" I asked.

He looked at me as though I was stupid. "It's all safe, moron."

"Says who?"

He didn't answer. He kept chewing, stuffing more seaweed into his mouth.

"How do you *know* it's safe?" I asked him again. But he still didn't tell me. I was so hungry that I didn't *care* if the seaweed made me sick. I plucked out a wrinkled leaf and started eating, and once I'd started I couldn't stop. Some of the seaweed was crunchy. Some was soft and slimy, and it slithered down my throat like globs of snot. All of it tasted awful, but I gorged myself anyway.

Frank gazed out at the sea and across the little cove. Then he turned to me and asked, still chewing, "Where's Jack?"

The question sort of stunned me. I was afraid to tell him the truth in case he fell into his eerie sleep again, or in case he refused to move until I'd answered a hundred questions. So I told a shameful lie. "He's gone ahead to look for help."

"Then let's find him." Frank stood up. He looked around again, down at my feet. "Hey, where are your shoes?"

"I lost them," I said.

"Moron."

The cliffs were less than twenty feet high, but the rocks were sharp and jagged. With cuts on my hands, and nothing but socks on my feet, I climbed a lot slower than Frank. But he didn't try to help me. He just scrambled up and disappeared over the edge.

By the time I reached the top I was sure he would be miles ahead. But he was lying on his back on a bit of grass, with a dried stem stuck in his teeth.

I had never imagined we would find people just beyond the cove. But it was still a huge disappointment to look to the north and see empty wilderness stretching on forever. If we had come to an island it was enormous, too big to walk around, too mountainous to cross. If we'd landed on the mainland, we might have to trek a thousand miles to find another person. It seemed useless to go on, but just as useless to stay where we were.

"How far did we go before we sank?" I asked.

Frank didn't answer.

"How long were we sailing?"

He still ignored me. He spat out the grass stem and flicked his hair. "Jack's dead, isn't he?" he asked.

I couldn't admit it so bluntly. I just nodded.

"Why didn't you tell me the truth?"

"I don't know," I said. "I was trying to help."

Frank glared at me. "The day I need your help, that's the day I kill myself."

Well, I had already saved his life. But I didn't point that out. Frank got up and started walking. A moment later, he whirled around and shouted at me, "Do you *know* he's dead?"

"Yes," I told him. "I saw it."

"You saw *what*?"

27

I felt tears coming into my eyes, so I turned away. "He was in the boat when it sank," I said. "He was right in front of me, down in the cabin."

"Then why didn't you save him?"

I looked up and stared right back, not caring now if my eyes were red. "Why didn't *you* save him?" I said.

"I would have," said Frank. "If I'd been that close."

"He told me to stay outside!" My hands were clenched so tightly that my fingernails pressed into the skin. "He went down to get the radio, and the water trapped him. What do you think I could do, you stupid idiot?"

"You could have tried," said Frank.

I shrieked at him, "The boat was sinking!"

Just a few feet apart, we snarled like animals about to kill each other. My heart was pounding, and Frank was flushed with anger. But just as I thought he was going to hit me, he reached up and flicked his hair again. Then he turned toward the sea, and a little bit of a calm came over us.

"So what about the radio?" His back was toward me. "Did he get it? Did he call for help?"

"No," I said.

"Why not?"

I didn't want to tell him about my fumbled catch. But into my mind came an image of Uncle Jack in the sinking boat, and it didn't seem fair to tell less than the truth. "He got the VHF," I said. "He tried to toss it through the hatch. But I missed."

A little sound came from Frank. Because I couldn't see his face, I didn't know if he was angry or amused. When he slowly turned around I saw only that annoying sort of pout that hid all expression.

"You're such a moron," he said. "*I* would have caught it."

"You couldn't even move. You were like a zombie." I glared up at him. "Why were you on the boat anyway? How do you know my uncle Jack?"

Frank just shrugged.

"Who *are* you?"

I hated looking up at him. He stared back until I had to turn away. Then he laughed and said, "I'm your guardian angel, Chrissy. I've been sent to Earth to save you."

"Yeah, whatever."

I went on toward the north again, along the narrow strip between cliff and trees. But Frank barreled past and led the way. His jacket, still soaking wet, dripped water. His boots squelched with every step.

Oh, I envied his boots. My socks already had holes in the heels, and my toes poked out the front. Stones and roots jabbed into my feet. "We could take turns with those boots," I said.

"Yeah, I guess we *could*," said Frank. But he kept walking.

Where the cliffs jutted, we took shortcuts through the forest, down trails that deer had made. Frank liked to bend the branches and let them spring back at me, so I learned to stay a bit behind. He plucked berries from the bushes and shoved them in his mouth.

"You shouldn't eat those," I told him.

"Why not?"

"They could be poisonous."

He laughed his annoying laugh and kept eating.

"Didn't you ever hear of poisonous berries?" I asked.

A heavy branch snapped from his hand and swung toward me. "Didn't anyone ever show you the good ones? Didn't your dad do that?"

"No," I said.

"Why not?"

"I don't know." It was a stupid question. "He just didn't."

Frank grunted.

"You don't go grazing for berries in the city," I told him. "Where do *you* live?"

He wouldn't answer that either. But he was desperate to show he knew more than me. "The purple ones are salal," he said. "The red ones are huckleberries. So are the blue ones, I think."

He stopped and broke off a sprig of red berries. He peeled away a handful them and shoved them into his mouth. Juice dribbled down his chin as he held out the branch. "Try some," he said.

"I'll wait a bit."

"Moron." He shrugged and started walking. I watched him carefully, in case he began to stagger. But the foul taste of seaweed was still in my mouth, and I ached with hunger. So after a while I tried the berries. The salal tasted bitter, but the huckleberries were sweet and juicy. They took away my thirst, but I felt as hungry as ever.

Our clothes dried as we walked. Frank took off his jacket and carried it over his shoulder, and in the miles that passed we never said another two words. I watched with dread as the sun sank lower, and I wished that *my* father had been more like Frank's. No one had ever taught *me* how to find water on a cliff, or food in a forest.

When Frank stopped to drink from a little stream, I kept trudging along, thinking about things. The forest grew dark, and when I looked back, Frank was not there.

I called his name. But he didn't answer. I had no idea how far I'd gone without him. I started back—at a walk, and then a run—and I found Frank kneeling by the same stream. In front of him lay a little pile of twigs and moss. He was busy scraping sticks together.

"What are you doing?" I asked.

"What does it look like, moron?" He didn't even lift his head. "I'm making a fire."

"You could have told me you stopped," I said.

"Why?" he asked, still not looking up.

"Why not?" I said. "I got you to shore. I saved your life. We have to stay together."

"Why?" he asked again.

"'Cause that's what you're supposed to do!" I shouted.

"Why?"

I felt like picking up one of the stones from the river and bashing his stupid head. I plopped down on the grass and watched him.

I had always thought that lighting a fire would be pretty easy, but I had never seen anyone actually try. Though Frank rubbed the sticks furiously, I saw no spark or plume of smoke. He had a serious, stubborn look that was somehow sad to see.

His hands began to shake, and his teeth showed in a hard line. He hunched forward over the little shreds of moss and worked in sudden bursts that left him exhausted. At last he fell back, muttering to himself as he glared at the sticks.

I tried to encourage him. "It'll be nice to have a fire," I said.

What anger flashed over him! "Do you think you can do better?" he asked.

"No," I said. "That's not—"

"Anyone who thinks it's easy to start a fire in a rain forest doesn't have a clue." Frank picked up the sticks again.

The sky darkened. A swarm of blackflies came. Frank

swatted at them as he worked, then suddenly swept the moss away and threw the sticks aside. "We don't need a fire tonight," he said. "It's too hot."

Well, *he* was hot. He was sweating from his efforts, but I was already cold.

Frank pulled his jacket around himself like a little tent and huddled inside it, safe from the blackflies. I kept slapping at them as they whined all around me, and I shivered in my T-shirt and sweater. From the distance came the howling of wolves. More eerie for its faintness, the sound tingled through my nerves.

I didn't sleep until the sky began to brighten. Then, as soon as I closed my eyes, it seemed, Frank was standing beside me, kicking my sore feet. "Let's go," he said.

His fingers and lips were stained blue with huckleberry juice. But he didn't bring any berries for me, or give me a chance to find my own. He kicked me again, then started walking north. I had to scramble to follow him.

We stayed at the edge of the sea, sometimes high on sheer cliffs, sometimes down on little beaches of gravel or rock. Three or four times I looked at my watch and saw the hands frozen at 3:15. It was as though we were doomed to walk forever, with time never changing.

"Where are we going?" I asked Frank's back as we passed through a strip of trees. "What are we going to do?"

As always, he ignored me. We went another half a

33

mile, across a ridge and out again to the cliffs. Frank stopped and turned around. He looked angry. "Why are we going north?" he asked.

I shrugged. "What's the diff?"

"'What's the *diff*,'" he said, mocking me with a laugh. "What are you, eight years old?" Stiffened with salt, his hair hung over his eyes like a pirate's patch. "How do you know there's not a whole city just south of here?"

It was another question that I had no answer to. I said, "I don't think there's a city anywhere."

"You don't know that, moron."

"I saw the land from the boat," I said. "You didn't."

Frank crossed his arms. "Maybe we should split up. You go north, and I'll go south."

I didn't like that idea, and he knew it. He just wanted me to plead with him. But I had done that too often for schoolyard bullies to want to do it again. If I let him push me around once, it would never stop. He would just push harder the next time. I shrugged and said, "Whatever," and started walking north.

Frank didn't follow me. It would have been too embarrassing to turn around and trail along behind him like his puppy, so I kept going. After half a mile, I knew I'd made a big mistake.

Below me was a little beach covered with garbage. I decided to explore it, hoping to find a pair of shoes for my sore feet. Then I could climb again to the next point, turn around, and catch up with Frank. "There's nobody there," I'd tell him. "We have to go south." It was a clever plan; he would get what he wanted, but I wouldn't be giving up. It was what my father would have called a "win-win."

In Vancouver, I couldn't have walked a quarter mile on English Bay without finding a flip-flop, a sandal or a sneaker. Along with baseball caps and disposable lighters, they had seemed as common as clamshells. In Alaska, it was even better.

The beach was made of pebbles; I sank right into them, as though trudging through a bowl of marbles. Among the stranded logs I found the same sort of stuff I'd seen floating in the ocean and remembered Uncle Jack. *"It's all going to wash up on the shore one day."* I found bottles and buckets and the bones of a giant whale. I found *two* cigarette lighters that wouldn't work, and then a sandal for my right foot. It was so oversized that it might have belonged to Bozo the Clown. But I slipped it on, and soon I found a pink flip-flop with a little heart on the sole.

Proud to have solved at least one of my problems, I tackled the rocks at the end of the beach. I climbed up and up, until I came out on top of a cliff so high it made me dizzy. White gulls flew below me tipping in the wind, and I must have seen for a hundred miles, over forests and mountains with no sign of people.

At that moment I was absolutely certain we would

never find anyone to the north. I would have *wanted* to find Frank and head south. But a bigger, better beach lay before me now. Made of sand like golden sugar, it stretched for a mile along the shore, and the breakers tossed and gleamed. Standing high above it, I felt as though I owned all I could see.

I had stepped into my mother's favorite movie: *Robinson Crusoe*. I could picture the castaway in his ragged goatskins, looking over the ocean from a ridge on his lonely island. That movie always made my mother cry. "We're all of us castaways," she told me once. "We get thrown ashore on the rocks of life, but somehow we survive."

I looked back, down the hill that I'd climbed. Something was moving through the bushes, crawling up toward me.

Wolves, I thought. Too frightened to move, I just watched the bushes sway and toss; I heard the branches crackle. Then, in a break between two trees, Frank appeared.

He was hurtling up the slope—almost frantically, it seemed—as though something was chasing him. He pulled with his hands as he pushed with his feet, blundering through the bushes. Then he glanced up and saw me standing above him, and for a moment I thought he was going to turn back. He sank down into the bushes, then appeared again, and he started *walking* up the hill. When he reached me, he was breathing heavily.

"I looked for miles to the south," he said. "There's nobody there." He wiped sweat from his forehead. "We'll go north instead, so you can stop crying now, you little crybaby."

Well, I wasn't crying. It was Frank who had lost something, and we both knew it. He shouldered past me to lead the way, and I followed in my familiar place. But I didn't mind anymore. I had learned an interesting lesson: even Frank didn't want to be left alone in all that wilderness.

4

The Cabin

Three chairs are set out on the point, around the wooden saint. Of course we only need two, but I like to have the extra one. I imagine this is where we'll be sitting when someone comes to save us. He will be so surprised to see us alive that he will just stand and stare with his mouth open. I'll gesture toward the empty chair and say politely, "Hello. Won't you please sit down?"

I can picture it clearly, even what our rescuer will look like. He will have sandy-colored hair, and a brown cap and dark sunglasses.

That's the way I see him. If he ends up looking different, it doesn't matter. I sometimes imagine things so clearly that I convince myself they will happen.

Pinned to our fridge back home is my second-grade report card, signed by Mrs. Lowe. She wrote, *Christo-*

pher has a vivid imagination. I think he will be a great artist one day. Perhaps a writer. Underneath, she added a different thought. *Christopher has trouble making friends.*

I laugh now when I remember this. In our first days in Alaska, I thought I would *never* be friends with Frank.

• • •

It was late in the afternoon when we came down to the sandy beach.

I kicked off my pink flip-flop, only to find that the sand scraped my blisters like a cheese grater. I limped like an old man. But I was glad to be out of the woods and down from the cliffs. Along the mile-long beach, waves collapsed in creamy foam. A flock of sandpipers raced back and forth at the edge of the water, as though afraid to get their feet wet.

Frank walked where the sand was firm and damp, and his shadow stretched across the beach like a stick man. I stayed higher up, where thousands of logs, whitened by the sun, made a giant's boneyard.

It was such a wild place. In Vancouver, city workers raked the sand every day and rearranged the logs into perfect rows. My father would wear his suit to go beachcombing, his tie flapping in the wind. Sometimes he'd talk like a pirate: "Come along, matey, there's treasure for the finding." He would make a game of turning junk into pieces of eight, but I expected to find wooden chests brimming with gold, and always went home disappointed.

All the stuff that Uncle Jack had talked about lay scattered across the sand. We found fishing floats and tangles of rope, bottles and buckets and all sorts of plastic things. But everything was covered with barnacles and weeds, and most of it was smashed into pieces. We hurried from one thing to another, shrieking and pouncing like seagulls. For a little while we were just two kids having fun on a sandy beach. But then the things became depressing—the endless number of them, the stories they whispered. It was strange to think that all the junk had been important once to people who were probably dead.

I had seen the tsunami on TV, whole cities swept away, people running for their lives, people trapped in cars or perched on rooftops. I had seen the enormous masses of debris washed down flooded streets and out to sea. Now those same things lay scattered all around me.

I collected bottles to fill with water, and more shoes than I could ever wear. There was not one that matched another, but I found two that I liked, and I kept another four for spares, carrying them around my neck on bits of rope.

"Watch for lighters," said Frank, as though I wasn't already doing that. But there were fewer than I'd expected, and they were rusted and brittle, ruined by salt or sunlight. Though I could see butane still sloshing inside when I held them up, they were useless.

At the end of the beach, a rocky finger stuck out into the sea. Along its back—like hackles on a dog—stood a few tall trees that swayed in the wind. A bald eagle came soaring above them, and behind the eagle came a raven, shouting crow-like cries. It swooped at the eagle's head, turned and swooped again, herding that huge bird through the sky.

Frank stopped to watch them pass. Then he sat on a log near the end of the beach.

If he was settling down for the night, he wouldn't say so. Not Silent Frank. So I kept walking, thinking I would cross the narrow point and see what lay ahead. I stayed among the logs until I saw an animal trail leading up through the bushes. Then I ducked under the drooping branches of a half-fallen tree, and stood again to step over the last log.

And I stopped with my foot in midair.

Pressed into the sand right in front of me was a human footprint.

It wasn't freshly made. The edges had crumbled, and a few brown tree needles had collected inside it. Shielded from wind and rain, it might have lasted for a long time, like footprints on the moon. But for sure it must have been made after the winter storms had passed. Sometime in the spring or the summer, someone had walked along the beach just as I had. He had crawled under the branches and stepped over the log, heading for the trail through the forest.

I shouted at Frank, "Somebody's here!" Then I followed the man's forgotten shadow, stumbling in the sand because I hurried. I sprawled facedown in his old footprint, got up and ran to the head of the trail. There, in the black dirt of the forest, I found another footprint preserved in hardened mud.

My mysterious man had hacked his way through the forest with an ax or a knife. His trail was overgrown with salal bushes, and I had to force my way through. I passed huge trees that must have been centuries old, and came to a small cabin in a clearing—a tiny house in the woods.

Held down with ragged bits of fishing net, a sheet of clear plastic covered the driftwood-shingle roof. Another square of plastic made a pane for a small window, but it was boarded over with scraps of wood. The cabin felt empty and forgotten. It felt haunted.

"Hello?" I called. "Hello?"

There was no sound from the surf, no sound from the wind, but breathy puffs of air made the plastic ripple on the roof like the skin of a breathing creature.

As I rounded the cabin's corner I saw the door was partly open. It had hung on hinges made of rope, but two were ripped apart, and the door sagged like a broken arm, swinging in the wind as though trying to close itself.

I held my shoes and water bottles in one hand, I put my head around the door and staggered back in surprise.

A huge black raven hung upside down in the doorway, bound in loops of red wire. It swung in front of me, turning slowly.

I had never been so close to a raven. Nearly as big as a Thanksgiving turkey, it must have stood almost two feet high. But its feathers were tattered, and the poor bird looked as ancient as a mummy. As it turned I saw the back of its head, where the feathers were ruffled and matted. I saw its beak. I saw its face.

It had no eyes. I gazed right into empty holes. But in a ring around each gaping socket, where the feathers were tiny and sparse, the skull showed in a white line that made it seem as though the raven was staring at me.

I heard Frank coming up the trail, thrashing his way through the bushes. He came in a huge rush, eager to see what I'd found. With his jacket fluttering behind him, he sprinted across the clearing. He ran right up to the cabin, pushed me aside, and wrenched the door wide open.

The dead raven whirled on its wire.

To Frank, it must have seemed that something had

leapt from the cabin to get him. He nearly screamed as he raised an arm to shield himself. Black and ragged, the raven hurtled toward him, then turned away and swooped again.

Behind us, another raven appeared. With a whistle of wings, it came flying through the trees, like a small shadow broken loose from the larger ones. It settled onto a branch that bent with its weight, then carefully folded its wings and tilted its head to look down.

Clearly embarrassed by his fright, Frank swore at the dead raven. He snatched a stick from the ground and hit it. The bird reeled across the doorway, spinning on the end of the wire. It swung into the cabin and out again, and above us the watching raven began to clamor and shout.

Frank grunted as he raised the stick and brought it down. Little feathers fluttered all around, and the dead bird spun faster while the living one screamed in the treetops. Then the wire broke, and that black corpse tumbled to the ground. Instantly, the screaming stopped.

It was brutal and quick, and in silence Frank poked the dead bird off to the side. He rolled it through the dirt and booted it into the bushes. Then he wiped his hands and went inside. I followed him.

The cabin was small and dark, with a rickety table and a rickety chair that had both fallen on their sides. A bed was built along one wall, its foam mattress pulled down to the floor at one corner. In the middle of the room was a fire circle made of stones. There were still ashes inside it, and the blackened ends of burnt sticks. Some of the stones had been rolled out of place, and someone had raked his fingers through the ashes, leaving long gouges that stretched toward the door.

Whoever had the built the cabin had meant to stay a long time. It was roofed for winter and shaded for summer. But in the end he had left in a hurry. I felt like a grave robber as we rummaged through the things left behind. We claimed them for ourselves: a camp stove and a bottle of gas to fuel it; a fork and spoon; a tin plate; a pot but no lid; a tiny lantern with a candle stub inside it.

"Look for food," said Frank. "There's got to be food somewhere."

I pulled the mattress off the bed and found only a nest that mice had built. Frank kicked apart a pile of driftwood sticks, then dropped to his knees and looked under the bed. He reached in and pulled out big sheets of plastic that were ragged and torn, an empty bucket, a bit of wood. Then he looked again and shouted, "Yes!" and reaching even farther, brought out a dozen ziplock bags. They'd been labeled with a red Sharpie: rice, coffee, raisins. But each one had been nibbled open by mice or rats, and all of them were empty.

Frank turned instantly from happy to furious. He hurled the bags onto the bed and looked around the little cabin. "See what's up there," he told me, pointing to a shelf high on the wall.

I climbed onto the bed, reached up and ran my hand along the shelf. Down fell a toothbrush and toothpaste, a roll of toilet paper in another ziplock bag, and then a small black box that bounced off the mattress and landed in the ashes.

We stared at that thing, for a moment too surprised to speak.

Frank snatched it up. He held it tightly, as though he had captured an animal that might try to struggle away.

"It's a radio," I cried.

"No kidding, Marconi."

It was almost exactly the same as the one that Uncle Jack had tossed to me in his last moment. "Here, let me try it," I said.

I jumped down from the bed, but Frank turned aside to shield the radio. He pressed a button on top, and a red light came on. Numbers lit up on a small gray screen.

We looked at each other, and for one instant we were a team, bound together by that radio and all that it offered.

Frank licked his lips. He lifted the radio up to his mouth. He pressed the transmitter. "Mayday," he said. "Mayday. Mayday."

He let go of the button. We both kept staring at the radio. A faint crackling came from the speaker.

"Squelch," I said, mimicking what Uncle Jack had taught us. "Turn the—"

"Shut up," snapped Frank. "I know what I'm doing." He turned the knobs for squelch and volume, and the sound became a roaring hum. Then he called again, "Mayday. Mayday."

A woman answered. Her voice was faint and crackly, but oh so wonderful. "Station calling Mayday: this is U.S. Coast Guard radio."

I grinned at Frank; he grinned at me. Both of us grinned at the radio. We were like a pair of chimpanzees, all teeth and foolishness. The woman's voice shattered with static. "What is the nature of your emergency?"

"Tell them our names!" I shouted at Frank. "Tell them we're lost."

"Shut up." Frank pressed the button again and spoke into the radio. "We need help. We're—"

The radio beeped. The numbers went out; the screen turned black. The little red light faded away, and the radio switched itself off.

Frank pressed every button; he turned every dial. Then he swore and hurled the radio across the cabin. It smashed against the wall. The back cover flew off; a battery ricocheted under the bed.

"Piece of junk!" shouted Frank.

"It's not the radio; it's the batteries," I told him.

"Who cares? It's still useless!" He gave me a furious

look, as though I was the one who had drained the batteries. "It's all junk. A stove without matches." He sent *that* flying across the room too. "A candle you can't light." *Wham* went the candle in its little holder. Then he folded his arms and dropped to the bed, pouting like a two-year-old.

I felt just as angry. I wished we had never found the radio, that we had never found the cabin. It was worse to have had our hopes raised so high and dashed again. But I started picking up the things that Frank had scattered. I had to crawl under the bed to chase the parts from the radio.

"Leave it," said Frank. "You're wasting your time."

"There might be spare batteries," I said.

Frank snorted. "And spare matches?"

"Why not?" I backed out from the under the bed. "If the guy had a stove, he must have had matches."

"Look in the spare room," said Frank.

Well, of course there was no other room. Frank was just trying to annoy me again, and he was getting pretty good at it. But I believed there had to be a box of matches somewhere, and probably another battery. So I set the rickety chair on the bed and peered over the edge of the shelf.

"There's *something* up here," I said. "There's a couple of things, I think."

The first was a book, an old paperback with pages coming loose. *Kaetil the Raven Hunter*, a novel by Daniel J.

Chesterson. On the cover was an unbelievably muscular man wearing animal skins, and on his shoulder perched a raven with a black hood, its talons tipped with silver spikes.

I read the blurb on the back aloud.

Left as a baby to die on a mountainside, Kaetil was rescued by ravens. Taught to hunt like a raptor, to think like a bird of prey, he grew up with one ambition: to find the man with yellow eyes. The man who'd killed his father.

"That sounds pretty good," said Frank. "What else is up there?"

I looked again. At the very back of the shelf was a box made of orange plastic. Frank snatched it from my hands and flicked the little latches. "A bunch of junk," he said, and dropped it on the mattress.

I got down and picked up the box again. Inside was a whole survival kit: a space blanket made of shiny foil; a whistle with a tiny compass fitted into the tip; a small mirror with a clear hole in the middle. There was a metal tube the size of a pen that I held up for Frank to see.

"Yeah, so *what?*" he said.

"It's a flare gun," I told him.

"You think I don't know that?" He was so angry that he looked ugly. "There's *nothing* you know that I don't know."

"But there's a flare too." I held it up, a little red cylinder.

Frank's voice broke into a squeak. "Who *cares?*" He swept his hand across the mattress, sending the whistle flying. "You moron. You think you can go out there and shoot off a flare and somebody's going to come and save us?"

"Why not?" I said.

"Because *NOBODY'S THERE!*"

I tried not to let him bother me. "The world's not all that empty," I said. "There's ships and planes and stuff, and somebody's going to come by. They're probably searching for us already."

"Don't be stupid," said Frank. "It'll be weeks before they even know the boat's missing. They won't have a clue where to look. There are thousands of miles, and they can't search every inch. It would take forever."

"So what do you want to do?" I asked.

"*So whaddya wanna do?*" he said, mocking my voice. "I want you to die, that's what I want."

That made me feel cold and small and awful inside. I was standing there like a butler, holding the flare and the little gun, and I didn't think I could take much more of Frank. I dropped the things on the bed and went outside.

The raven shouted at me.

He had dragged the dead bird from the bushes and was hunched over it now. Stuck in his beak were tiny black feathers. He thrust out his head, puffed his wings and shrieked at me.

He seemed a cruel thing, a little cannibal busily chewing away at his dead companion. He had covered the ground with bits of red insulation pulled from the wire. It was obvious that he was telling me to keep away, so I held up my hands as I stepped around him. "Okay," I said. He swiveled his head to watch me with his black eyes.

To my left was the trail coming up from the beach. To my right, another path led into the bushes. The branches on either side nearly met in the middle, but I could see that the trail had been used many times. There was a rut worn into the ground.

I took that trail through the forest. Twisting between the trees, it led me toward the narrow finger I had seen from the beach, the sound of surf growing louder. I came out onto a small meadow surrounded on three sides by the sea. Yellow grasses bent in the wind, and a lonely tree stood black and gaunt against the clouds. Storms had shaped its trunk into a twisted cord, its branches into spidery fingers. Black with age, almost bare of needles, it looked like a crippled old woman, a hag dressed in fluttering shreds of moss.

Squinting against the glare of the setting sun, I saw four wooden boxes set in the crooks of the branches.

Made of cedar planks, they looked nearly as old as the tree. Spotted with lichen, turned silver by sunlight, they were slowly disintegrating. Two had split open; their ends had caved in. I could see leg bones and ribs inside, and the round top of a skull. They were coffins.

In the red light of the sunset, I felt a cold chill. I thought of the skeletons sleeping together in their separate boxes, like astronauts in a spaceship or something. I backed away slowly, through the shadow of the tree where it sprawled across the grass. Then I turned and ran to the cabin.

The raven was still on the ground, tearing now at the wire that bound the corpse. Again he raised his head and spread his wings. He opened his beak so wide that I could see his tongue inside, a little orange dart. He made a strange sound that rattled from his chest, as though he was trying to speak.

He was big enough to seem threatening. I was wondering how to get around him when Frank came up the trail from the sandy beach. At that moment, the raven lifted into the air and flew away between the trees.

Frank was angry. "Where did you go?" he said.

"Out there," I told him, pointing down the other trail. "There's a tree with coffins in it. And there's skeletons inside them."

He looked doubtful. "Show me," he said.

"It's nearly dark," I told him.

"So what?" He tossed his hair aside. "You scared?"

I hated the way he smirked. Yes, the skeletons had scared me. But I wouldn't admit it. "Let's go," I said.

By the time we reached the meadow, the sun had gone down. Beyond the forest, a jagged mountain rose like a crouched giant, and the skeletons rested unseen in their boxes, under a purple sky.

Frank stepped toward the tree. I had a sudden fear that he would break off a branch and start bashing at the skeletons.

But he was solemn and serious. He walked twice around the tree without speaking, his feet shuffling in a slow funeral march. Then he stopped, with his hands on his hips, and stared up at the coffins. The highest one was so small that it must have held a child. A lower one had broken open, and scraps of cloth hung from the box like cobwebs. I saw the skeleton inside, stretched out on its back with its skull tipped sideways, as though staring across the sea.

Frank went closer, but I wouldn't move. He noticed, and laughed. "You *are* scared," he said.

"No," I told him. "It's just creepy."

"Why?" said Frank. "It's just a cemetery. There's so much rock and stuff, this is how the Indians used to bury people. They're just old bones."

"That used to be people."

"So what?" Frank tossed his head. "Everybody dies. I'd rather be put in a tree than buried in the ground. Who wants to be eaten by worms?"

"Who wants to be pecked by birds?"

Frank shrugged in his annoying way. He went right

up to the tree and touched its black bark. He ran his hand along the trunk.

"What sort of tree is that?" I asked.

Frank stared up through the branches. He looked at me, then walked away. "It's a skeleton tree, moron."

The wind was fading, the sea becoming calm. Waves breathed up against the shore, and a seagull cried as it flapped its way home. But these were sounds I barely noticed anymore, a background hum like traffic in the city, so I heard quite clearly the little scratch and shuffle that came from the tree. In the fading wind, it could not have been a creak of branches. It was something scraping on wood, something scratching.

As I turned to follow Frank, I noticed something strange. In the shadows of the open coffin I could see the skeleton's gaping eyes. It had turned its head to peer down at me.

5

The Raven

Even now, weeks later, I still feel a prickly chill when I think of the skeletons.

I've had nightmares trying to figure them out. Why are there coffins up in a tree? Could the tsunami have tossed them there? Were people put in the coffins alive and left to die? Did they climb up there themselves?

Or maybe Frank is right. Maybe once, long ago, a village stood along the sandy beach, and the tree is just a graveyard in a land with a lot of rock but not much dirt. Maybe the most important people were put to rest in the branches of the skeleton tree. That makes more sense.

But I can't get it out of my mind that the skeletons come down in the night. I've imagined them lifting the lids of their coffins, peering out at the twilight, then clambering down to run through the forest.

What's that sound behind me? If I turn around now will I see the skeletons climbing back to their places? I can imagine one swinging his long bones over the edge of the box, sliding into his coffin like a fighter pilot into his cockpit.

I will be glad to be away from here. But I don't think I'll ever forget the skeletons. They'll appear in my dreams for as long as I live.

· · ·

I knew it that first day, when Frank left me alone at the skeleton tree. He went away without telling me, and I looked back to see him already at the far side of the clearing, nearly at the forest. "Wait up!" I shouted.

He laughed and kept going.

I started running. As I stumbled across the grass, Frank looked over his shoulder and saw me. He started running too. He vanished down the black mouth of the trail.

It pleased me to think that he was at least a little bit frightened. But that wasn't true; Frank was only planning ahead. He didn't care about skeletons; he had only hurried away to claim the only bed.

By the time I arrived in the cabin he was already sprawled across the foam mattress. The orange box and all its contents were dumped on the floor.

I felt stung, but there was nothing I could do. I managed to pull the door shut and wedge it in place, but the old wooden latch was broken. The boarded window made the cabin as black as a tomb, and I had to feel my way to the corner, where I settled down on the bare floor. I fell asleep in a moment, only to snap awake again. Something was moving outside.

"Did you hear that?" I asked. "Frank! Did you hear that?"

Half-asleep, already annoyed, he growled at me, "Hear *what*?"

"That sound."

"What sound?"

It came again, a tiny scratching. "There!"

"It's nothing," said Frank. "Go to sleep."

"I think there's something out there," I said.

"There's *always* something out there," said Frank. "It's the forest."

The bed creaked as he rolled heavily onto his side. To him, that was the end of it. I lay back again on the floor, but I couldn't possibly sleep. I lay still and straight, listening for every sound. But nothing moved.

"Frank? Are you asleep?" I asked.

He groaned. "Yes, Chris, I'm asleep."

I tried to speak to him nicely. "You think we're going to get home?"

He said nothing.

"I think we will. I bet boats go by all the time. Float-planes too. We might even see one tomorrow."

Frank was lying quietly on the bed.

"We could take turns watching," I said. "If we see a boat or a plane, we can shoot off the flare."

He didn't even grunt.

"Or we could use the flare to start a fire. Hey, why not?" I said. "A fire would keep us warm. It would be a signal too. I mean, if you can't start a fire with—"

"I *know* how to start a fire," said Frank. "I told you that, moron. Now shut up and go to sleep."

For a while I lay silently below him. Then I said, "Frank? Just—"

"Shut up."

"Just tell me one thing," I said. "Do you want to stay here in the cabin? Or do you want to keep going north?"

No answer.

"Frank, what do you want to do?"

"Sleep," he said. And he did. Soon he was snoring softly, and the sound was a comfort.

Morning came in slits of gray light through the boarded window, through the doorframe, even through little chinks in the cabin walls. Cold and uncomfortable, I groaned as I got up from the floor. Frank was awake, just lolling on the foam pad with his jacket for a blanket. He watched me walk toward the door.

"Where are you going?" he asked.

"To look for ships," I said.

"Look for water," he told me. "That's more important. Or look for food." He tossed the jacket aside and sat up. "Go get some seaweed."

I didn't like being bossed around. "Go get some yourself," I said.

"All right, Chrissy," he said with pretended patience. "I was *going* to get a bunch of clams or something. But if you'd rather do that, go ahead."

He knew exactly how to annoy me. He used just the right tone and just the right words, and he knew very well that I didn't have a clue about clams. "Forget it," I said.

I shoved the door to go out, and it fell back on its last hinge, slamming into the ground. Again I saw the raven peering up at me from the body of his dead friend. As surprised as me, he thrashed his wings and soared over my head, up to the cabin roof. He rocked from one foot to the other. The feathers on his back were ragged and out of place, and he looked like a worried little man. When I crouched over the dead bird, he began to mewl sadly. When I picked it up, he howled.

"It's okay," I told him.

As large as it was, the dead bird weighed almost nothing. It felt hard and hollow, dried out like an old gourd. As I held it, Frank appeared. His hair was spiky and disheveled, like the feathers of the raven, and when he saw me he grimaced. "That thing's probably loaded with lice," he said.

I dropped it. Frank stepped forward and kicked it

into the bushes. On the rooftop, the raven screamed. Frank paid no attention. "You won't find seaweed in the forest," he said as he walked past me.

The raven on the roof muttered and cooed. I could see the dead bird lying upside down in the bushes. So I found a stick and pulled it out again. I scraped out a little grave from the moss and the dirt.

The raven's cries grew louder. He swung his head and slashed his beak across the plastic. He *moaned.* I remembered standing over my father's grave at the huge cemetery on a hillside, hearing my mother cry beside me. The way I'd felt then, that was the sound the raven was making.

I placed the dead bird gently in its shallow hole, and was about to cover it over when I thought of the skeleton tree. *Who wants to be eaten by worms,* Frank had asked. Not a raven, for sure. I lifted the bird out of the ground and carried it down to the point. From the roof, the raven rose to follow me, and when I reached the clearing he was already perched at the top of the skeleton tree. For him, it was just a place to look out across the sea and the land. The skeletons meant nothing to a raven; for him there was no fear of death and old bones.

It was a day with no wind, a day that felt like the end of summer. Small, high clouds dotted a sky of watery blue, and the ancient coffins looked like little boats floating on a great wide sea.

As the raven watched, I unwrapped the red wire

and hung it in a loop around my neck. I was shocked to see the deep ruts in the bird's feathers and body. But its wings fell open, and I thought I'd set the raven free. Reaching up as high as I could, I placed the poor dead thing into a crook of the branches.

I didn't mean to look in the boxes. But the movement of a tattered cloth caught my eye, and I suddenly found myself staring right up through the rotted floor of a coffin, at the same skeleton that had looked down at me the night before.

I saw shreds of moss clinging to a skull that had turned up toward the sky again.

The wind had moved it, I told myself. But I couldn't remember any wind.

I ran to the end of the point. The tide was so high that most of the seaweed was underwater, but I found a few pieces of brown kelp cast up among the stones. I tore off the long leaves and took them back to the cabin. I didn't even glance at the skeleton tree.

Frank came in right after me, carrying an old bucket that he plunked down in the middle of the floor. He chose two sticks from the scattered firewood and squatted down to start a fire. I peered into the bucket at a squirming mass of Frankenstein creatures, half plant and half animal. "What are those?" I asked, disgusted.

"What do you think?" said Frank.

I had no idea. I shook the bucket to make the creatures tremble. Frank had said he was getting clams, but these weren't clams. They had bulbous heads that looked like claws, and short, stubby bodies, and they twisted and twitched in a way that didn't seem normal. I thought of the nuclear reactors destroyed by the tsunami. "Are they mutants?" I asked.

Frank snorted. He rubbed the sticks so quickly that his hands moved in a blur. But no smoke or flame appeared. Just as he had last time, he soon lost patience and threw the sticks away. "Forget it!" he shouted. "We can eat them raw."

"But what are they?" I asked.

He almost screamed at me. "Gooseneck barnacles, you moron!" Then he came and grabbed the bucket. When he looked inside, his expression almost made me laugh. I thought he was going to vomit. "They stick on to stuff way out at sea," he said. "Mostly they're dead when you find them. I never really ate them before."

"What happened to the clams?" I asked.

"High tide, moron."

I had never gone digging for clams, but even I knew that you couldn't do it if the beach was underwater. I watched Frank pull one of the barnacles from the bucket. He held its claw pinched in his fingers as it writhed like a maggot.

It had brown skin as wrinkled as an elephant's trunk. With a little tearing sound, Frank peeled that away. The flesh underneath was yellow. Frank grimaced. Then he shoved the thing into his mouth, bit off the fleshy head and dropped the claw in the bucket. He wiped his mouth with his hand.

"Not bad," he said.

I laughed. His face looked sour and disgusted.

"No, really," he said. Then both of us laughed, and the yellow goo of the barnacle bubbled up in his mouth. It was gross and disgusting, but the first nice moment we had ever had together.

He ate a second barnacle, and then a third before I tried one myself. It was salty and rich, and I hated the idea that it was still alive. The feel of it sliding down my throat nearly made me gag. But the taste wasn't all that bad.

Frank watched as I swallowed. "Well?" he asked.

"It's not the worst thing I ever ate," I said. "Once, when I was a kid, I ate dog droppings."

Frank laughed. "I ate glass."

"Really? What happened?" I said.

"I don't remember exactly," said Frank. "But it was scary. My mom freaked out and called nine-one-one. They came and fed me cotton wool."

"Why?" I asked.

"To pad the glass, I guess." Frank shrugged. "It made me cry; I remember that."

It was strange to think of Frank crying. He started telling me more, then suddenly stopped, as though he'd said too much already. But we kept eating the barnacles. We finished the whole bucket, laughing together as we did silly things. I arranged four in my hand as though they were fingers. Frank dangled two from his head like alien tentacles. In that little cabin, in that lonely land, we were happy.

"Hey, Frank?" I said.

"Yeah?" He looked up, smiling.

"Why did Uncle Jack take you sailing?"

It was as though a door suddenly closed between us. I could almost hear it slamming shut. The smile vanished from Frank's face. A half-finished barnacle drooped from his fingers.

"I don't want to talk about that," he said. His voice was so cold that it scared me. "I'm glad he's dead, and that's all."

Frank stood up. He dropped the barnacle into the bucket and went out to the forest. With nothing else to do, I cleaned up the cabin. I folded the plastic sheets and pushed them under the bed. I set up the table, sorted the firewood, placed the stones in a circle again. When Frank came back I was down on my hands and knees with the red wire still around my neck, trying to find the pieces from the radio. He stepped right over me and threw himself down on the bed.

The silence felt awful. I didn't want to be the first to speak, but I imagined us both being so stubborn that we never talked again. A picture came to my mind of the two of us ancient and bearded, just sitting and staring at each other. It made me laugh.

"What's so funny?" said Frank.

"Nothing," I said.

"Then why did you laugh, moron? You laughing at *me*?"

"No," I said. It seemed strange that he cared about that. I didn't think people like Frank even imagined that people might be laughing at them.

I couldn't find the knob for the radio. So I took the paperback book, *Kaetil the Raven Hunter,* and sat in the chair to read it. The pages were yellow, all bent and smudged. The book must have been read a hundred times. It opened right at the beginning, as though the cabin guy had trained it.

I started reading. But right away, Frank interrupted. "What are you doing?" he asked.

"What does it look like?" I said. "I'm reading a book."

"Can't you do something useful?"

I had heard the same words a thousand times from my father. Just as he might have done, Frank got up and slapped the book from my hands. "Come on," he said. "You can hunt for treasure."

I'd heard that too. With that same promise of treasure, I would have gone with my father to English Bay. Now I followed Frank through the forest, along a trail that took us north to a stream of cold water. It burbled down tiny waterfalls into a pool as round as a barrel. Frank dropped to the ground and dunked his face right into the water. We had not had a drink since the day before. But I still drank like a timid animal, lifting water in my hands as I kept a watch on the forest.

Though the water was so cold that it hurt my teeth, Frank washed his face and his precious hair, splashing silvery drops in the sun. As I gazed all around, I saw a red-handled jackknife lying near the trunk of a tree. I ran to get it, my fear suddenly forgotten. "A knife!" I shouted.

"Let me see," said Frank.

The blade was open and stained with streaks of brown. "It's kind of rusty," I said.

"Come on, let's see!" Frank stood up and held out his hand. I knew that if I didn't give him the knife right then I'd be wrestling him for it a moment later. So I passed it over, to save some time and pain.

Frank tossed it in his palm. He closed the blade and opened it again, then held it near his eyes.

"I don't think that's rust," he said.

He dipped the knife into the pool and cleaned the blade with his fingers. Little swirls of red drifted away. To me, it seemed creepy: first an empty cabin, now a bloodstained knife. But Frank had a simple answer.

"This is where the cabin guy would have cleaned his fish and stuff. Maybe rabbits," he said. "It's lucky he dropped the knife."

I watched Frank flick the blade open and shut. "Okay, give it back now," I said.

"It's not yours," said Frank. "It's the cabin guy's."

"Yeah, well, if he comes back, I'll give it to him."
I held out my hand and wiggled my fingers. "Give it back."

Frank tossed his wet hair. Then he smiled and held out the knife—until I reached out to take it. Then he snatched it away, slipped it into his pocket and walked on down the trail.

"Oh, that's nice," I said. "That's real nice." I felt I could have killed him just then, and I muttered awful things behind his back.

But I forgot my anger as we walked deeper into the forest. Moss grew thick and heavy, covering every hump and hollow, every fallen log. Where we walked it sprang right up behind us, and we left no tracks; we made no sound. The trees soared straight as columns, then suddenly spread out in a shimmering roof of green and gold seven stories high. No logger had ever been there, and the trees might have lived a thousand years.

We didn't talk as we walked through the forest, and then for another mile along cliffs of staggering height. Then the land sloped down to a gravel beach. And there, among stranded logs and enormous boulders, we found a fishing boat.

The Edge of Our World

Something has gone very wrong.

Of all the things I've imagined, I never once thought of fog. But far to the north and out to the west, the sea is hidden by a thick, white blanket.

A voice whispers doubts in my ear. *Nobody's coming. It was only a dream.* How will anyone find us if our world shrinks to a gray circle?

I shout aloud, trying to drive away the thoughts, "Today is the day! This is the day we'll be saved!"

Just off the shore a seal pops its head from the sea and stares at me with enormous eyes. It must think I'm crazy to be screaming at the sky. But I've told Frank that if we have any doubts, it will not happen. If we *believe* we'll be saved, we'll be saved.

I keep chanting: "Today is the day. Help's on the way."

I repeat it over and over, until the words become a senseless jumble. But the fog is growing thicker. I can see it spreading south.

I glance back at the meadow, at the trees and the dark bushes. If Frank appears now he might lose hope. He might blurt out words that will ruin everything.

On the grass beside my favorite chair are the drums we've made from a bucket and a metal barrel. I sit, take up the sticks and start to beat a rhythm on the barrel. It's a savage sort of sound that rumbles out across the sea.

Boom-boom, boom, boom-boom. My arms move like levers. The sticks bounce up from the drum. I drive them down again. *Boom, boom, boom-boom.* Frank would not believe me, but I can drum the fog away.

I pound on the drum, but the fog keeps rolling closer. I can imagine it creeping along the shoreline, covering the river, swallowing the boulders, filling the old boat with a cold, gray gloom.

• • •

When I first saw that boat I thought we were saved.

It sat upright among the logs, like a bird in a fabulous nest. I thought we could drag it down to the water and sail away, and I ran toward it.

But when I got a bit closer I saw that the boat was a wreck. A log had pierced the cabin windows—in the back and out the front. Like a huge wooden nail, it pinned the boat to the land. Shattered glass lay everywhere.

A name was still painted on the bow, though it had nearly faded away. *Reepicheep.* Frank frowned as he touched the letters. "What the heck does that mean?"

"It's a mouse," I told him. "Reepicheep was a warrior, the bravest mouse in Narnia, and—"

"Who cares?" said Frank. He slipped around behind the boat, then appeared on the deck, popping up between the logs.

The boat gave me a feeling of sadness, and I didn't go any closer. I stood fiddling with the raven's red wire while Frank explored the places where the fisherman had lived and worked, and maybe died. He crawled right inside the wreck, through a narrow gap between the planks and the gravel. I could hear him shouting that the engine was still in the boat, that he'd found a jigging line, that he'd found a gaff.

When he came out he was happy. The gaff was stout and heavy, a club with a hook on the end. The jig was a pink lure wrapped with fishing line around a rusted bolt.

Frank nodded toward the wreck. "That was his boat."

"Whose boat?" I asked.

"The cabin guy!" cried Frank. "Who do you think, moron? He was shipwrecked."

"No," I said. "It's been here for ages."

Frank nodded. "So was the guy."

"Not for ten years!"

Frank echoed me, mockingly. "*Ten years.* Like you would know."

"Then how long do you think?"

He crossed his arms and studied the stranded boat. Waves pounded on the beach behind us. "A year," he said. "Maybe two."

It seemed crazy at first, but he might have been right. One long winter of snow and storms could have made the boat look ancient.

Frank stuffed the jig into his pocket and started north again. He let the gaff swing by its hook like a walking stick. The stones rolled under our feet, and a sound like rain moved along with us, as thousands of tiny crabs scuttled into hiding places.

Around the next bend, the beach was scattered with enormous boulders. The waves made a steady roar and rattle as they broke on the beach, and a great chunk of Styrofoam tumbled back and forth. Then the shoreline turned again, and we found ourselves at the mouth of a river. It tumbled out of the forest down a stony water-fall, into a vast pool of salt water. I could see salmon fins and tails slicing through the surface, their bodies gliding like shadows underneath.

That river would become the edge of our world. There was no point in trying to go farther. To the north was only more of what we'd already seen: more rocks, more forests, more sea and mountain. But I felt happy here. A cool breeze came down from the river, smelling of forest and fish. A rainbow made an arch above the falls, and the water cascaded from ledge to ledge in curls of creamy white. Salmon flung themselves against the waterfall, trying to struggle up the river.

It didn't seem possible that they could ever reach the top. But of course they would—or most of them would. They would fight their way right into the mountains, to the exact spot where they had been born, just to lay their eggs before they died. It was a beautiful thing to see, sad and brave at the same time.

But to Frank it meant nothing. He went straight to the pool, thrust the gaff into the water, and shaded his eyes to peer under the surface.

Through layers of color and patches of light, hundreds of fish swam around and around. There were so many that Frank could hardly miss, and in a moment he had one speared on the hook. He hauled the salmon out, a shining thing that thrashed so hard he could barely hold on. He swung it around and slammed it down on the stones. Using the gaff as a club, he hit it three times while it twisted on the ground. Blood and scales splattered on his clothes, his face and his hands. But he grinned as he held up the fish, so big that its tail nearly touched the ground. He tossed his hair aside. With sunlight mottled in the trees behind him, with the silver of the fish, it was as though the old photograph of my father had come to life. I remembered my mother smiling at the picture, and I wondered what she was doing right then. I wondered if I would ever get home to see her.

"Isn't that a beauty?" said Frank.

I saw how he strained to hold that heavy fish. "It sure is," I said. But I didn't sound enthusiastic, and his smile vanished. He dropped the salmon and started fishing again. It lay stiff at his feet, already not quite so shiny, as though the glistening brightness was part of its life, its spirit. Now it just looked dead, and the scales sparkled on the rocks instead, in a smear of slime and blood.

Frank didn't catch another. Maybe the fish were smarter. Or maybe he was trying too hard. He swished the gaff through the water, swearing whenever he missed.

7

The Airplane

In my hand the sticks leap and bounce on the drum top. *Boom, boom, boom, boom-boom.* I have kept the fog away, and I don't mind if it stays where it is. A whole fleet of ships could be hidden inside it, plowing toward me right now. At any moment they might appear, dragging tendrils of mist from their funnels and masts.

But I can't let the fog come closer. I beat harder and faster on the drum, sending the sound rolling across the sea like little peals of thunder.

Boom, boom, boom-boom.

In my mind I keep seeing Frank at the fishing pool, bashing at the water. More than six weeks since that day on the river, I can still see the expression on his face as he grew more and more frustrated.

∙ ∙ ∙

It made me sad to watch him. It made me think of my father, who loved to go fishing as a boy but for some reason gave it up. I never saw him with a rod and reel.

"Did *your* dad ever take you fishing?" I asked Frank.

He didn't know what I'd been thinking. He frowned for a moment, then said, "Sure. All the time. We went fishing and hunting and everything. I wish he was here now. He'd catch a *pile* of fish. He'd catch them with his bare hands."

"Not *my* dad," I said, laughing.

Somehow, even that made Frank angry. He stabbed the gaff into the pool and swore as he slashed it through the water.

"Let me try," I said.

"I can do it better than you," he told me.

"Then give me that jigging thing," I said.

"You'll lose it."

"Oh, come on," I told him. "How am I going to lose it?"

But I lost it. The stones by the pool were slick with salmon blood, and I slipped as I cast out the line. The rusted old bolt flew from my hands.

Frank heard it hit the water. He looked at the little splash out on the pool, and then at me, and very slowly he stood up. I was afraid he would beat me with the gaff, just the way he had bashed the salmon.

"I'm sorry," I said.

"That was our only hook. Do you have any idea . . ." Frank held up his hands. The veins in his neck looked like tightened ropes. "If we don't eat, we'll die."

"I know that," I told him. "I said I'm sorry."

He stepped so close that I could smell seaweed and sweat on his clothes. I stared back at him, frightened. But he only reached out and ripped the loop of wire from my neck, then walked away. He brought out the knife I'd found at the stream and gutted the fish he'd caught. He tied the red wire in a loop through the gaping cheeks of the salmon and hoisted the fish to his shoulder. "Let's go home," he said.

Home. I didn't like to think of that tiny cabin as home. My home was Vancouver, and I wanted so badly to be there.

Frank's silence felt worse than ever as we walked along. I wished he would talk, if only to tell me how stupid I'd been. I wished he would shout. But he didn't say a single word all the way to the cabin. And then he walked right past it, down the trail to the sandy beach.

"Where are you going?" I asked.

"We'll eat on the beach," he said.

"Like a picnic?"

He grunted. "Yeah, Chrissy. Like a picnic."

Well, it was no picnic. We ate seaweed that had just

washed ashore, still salty and wet and gritty with sand. Frank used the knife to hack slabs from the salmon carcass and we wolfed them down like cavemen, with blood and juice pouring over our hands and our wrists. We spat out the bones.

It was cold and awful, but I didn't want to disappoint Frank. "It's like sushi," I said.

He looked at me, but said nothing.

"You know what my dad used to say about sushi?" I asked. "'When I was a kid we called it bait.'"

A little glimmer came into Frank's eyes. He was careful not to smile, not to show emotion. He just nodded, as though at an old joke. But that encouraged me to keep talking. "My dad died a year ago," I said. "He was killed in an accident."

Frank's expression didn't change. He looked down the beach, out at the rows of breakers.

"He was an accountant," I said. Then, "So what does *your* dad do?"

Frank shrugged. "Not much."

I wiped my fingers in the sand. "Like what?"

"He lies around and decomposes."

It took me a moment to realize what that meant. And then it seemed a terrible way to put it. "I'm sorry," I said.

"Why?" Frank leaned back on his elbows. "Was it your fault?"

I gave up on pleasant conversation. I watched the

waves and thought of my father, remembering strange little things one after the other. When he came home from work he would fling open the door and hold up his hand and say, "Greetings, earthlings!" in a funny voice. When he went away on trips he would always bring back a present for me. But he would pretend that he hadn't, until he looked into his briefcase with a clown's look of surprise. "Oh, what's this in here?" he would say.

The memories suddenly dissolved when Frank spoke again.

"There's that raven," he said.

I saw a shadow flitter across the sand. Then the bird swooped behind us with a whistling sound in his wings. He landed on a log nearby, ruffled his feathers, and strutted back and forth.

"Hello," I said.

The raven scraped his black beak across the wood.

"Want some fish?"

I picked up a piece of the carcass. But Frank shouted at me, "No! Don't give him that."

"It's just the tail," I said. "*We're* not going to eat it."

"If you feed that thing, you'll never get rid of it."

"I don't *want* to get rid of him." The fish tail dangled from my hand, all speckled and bright. As it swung from my fingers the raven watched, his head swinging comically.

"He'll be a pest," said Frank.

"Not to me." I tossed the tail onto the sand, just below where the raven stood. He made a little warbling sound and watched suspiciously, but he didn't move until Frank got up and walked away. Then he hopped down and grabbed the salmon, and in the same motion flapped away into the sky.

As I watched him circle in front of me, a little speck of light appeared above the sea. I heard a rumbling sound, faint and far away.

I stood up. "An airplane!" I shouted. "Frank, there's an airplane!"

He was already looking at the sky, his hands like a visor on his forehead. "Where is it?" he cried.

The sound grew louder. I saw the dot of light again, already bigger. "There!" I pointed. "Right there."

Frank dashed away along the sand, heading for the cabin. I hurried after him in my crummy, floppy shoes, and by the time I reached the cabin he had been in and out already. He stood by the door holding the little flare gun.

He shook it at me. "Where's the flare?" he shrieked.

"In the box," I told him.

"Well, it's gone!"

The faint rumble had become a throbbing that I could feel in the air. I went past Frank and into the cabin. He had hurled the orange box onto the fire circle, where it lay with its lid cracked in two.

"Find the flare!" yelled Frank.

The jet was very close. Frank blundered through the room like a trapped bird, bouncing from wall to wall. He knocked over the table; he toppled the chair; and then he grabbed the signaling mirror from the ashes and barreled outside.

I ran after him, down the trail toward the skeleton tree. When we reached the clearing, the jet was nearly overhead. I saw the wings and fuselage glaring in the sunlight, a contrail streaming out across the sky.

I waved at the plane. I jumped up and down and shouted. "Do you think they can see us?" I asked.

"They're five miles up, you moron," said Frank.

He was aiming the mirror toward the plane, sighting through the clear, round spot in the middle. He was trying to reflect the sun into tiny windows five miles away, and he tilted the mirror this way and that.

But the jet was already gone. It was moving across the clearing, above the skeleton tree, on toward the forests and the mountains.

"Could they see the mirror?" I asked. "Frank, do you think—"

"How would I know?" he snapped. "Don't be stupid."

It felt strange to stand there and watch that airplane fly away, to think of the people inside it. I tried to imagine someone leaping up from a window seat, shouting, "There's someone in trouble down there! You gotta believe me."

But that didn't seem very likely.

The plane became a dot again and slowly faded away. The contrail began to break apart, turning red in the high sunset. Seeing it all vanish made me feel at the edge of the world in a different way. All the normal things were still going on, and would go on no matter what happened to Frank and me. There were seven billion people on Earth, and all but a handful were living their lives unchanged, without a thought or a care for us.

Frank looked so slumped and sad that I felt sorry for him.

"It might come again," I said. "Maybe there's a schedule."

"Yeah. Once a century," said Frank.

We went together down the trail, together to the cabin. Frank stepped right over all the things from the orange box and collapsed on the bed. He rolled himself up in the foam pad, using it as both a blanket and a mattress.

"I thought we were taking turns with the bed," I said.

"We are," he said. "When it's your turn, I'll tell you."

I jammed the door shut as I had the night before. I stuffed everything back in the plastic box except for the flare—which I couldn't find—and the space blanket—which I hoped would keep me warm. With the cabin guy's spoon I scraped two marks in the wall, to show that we had lived two days in the cabin. I wondered how many days would have to pass before I'd covered the whole cabin with notches. I imagined myself again as a bearded old man, gouging the last possible mark in the far corner, trying to remember what I was counting.

Frank watched from the bed, but didn't say anything.

I put the spoon on the table, opened the pouch and pulled out the space blanket. It looked and felt like a shiny garbage bag, just one thin layer of plastic that crackled as I spread it out. Disappointed, I pulled it over my feet and legs, up to my chin, and curled myself in the corner.

I wasn't as cold as I had been the night before, but I sure wasn't toasty. I shivered as I tried to sleep, and even *that* annoyed Frank.

"Stop crinkling!" he told me.

I slept off and on until dawn, when a shadow flitted past the slits of light in the cabin wall. Something tapped at the window.

I couldn't see anything between the nailed-up boards. The thing scratched at the plastic pane.

As loud as I dared, I whispered for Frank. The sounds stopped for a moment, then started again.

"Frank!"

He spluttered in his sleep, but didn't wake up. I whispered again.

And that thing outside began to talk.

It muttered words I couldn't understand. Its voice

wasn't human, or at least not alive. Through the window came a croaking hiss, like an old man's breathing.

Lousy birds.

I didn't care if Frank got angry. I scrambled out of the space blanket and shook him awake.

"Frank!" I shouted. "Frank!"

He woke with a gasp, then pushed me away. "Leave me alone," he said.

"Something's trying to get in," I told him.

"Oh, Chris."

"Just listen!" I said.

He lay back, glaring up at me. I saw his eyes shifting as he looked up across the ceiling, down toward the floor. "I don't hear anything," he said.

"Well, it's there," I told him. "It was pulling at the window. It was—"

Frank shoved me aside as he got up. He crossed the cabin, pushed open the door and stepped out. I held my breath, expecting that thing to come charging from the forest.

But whatever had been there was gone. Frank walked around the little cabin, and when he came back I felt about two feet tall, a frightened little kid. He looked at me as though I was a bug.

"It *was* there," I told him. "I heard it, Frank. It talked to me."

He flicked his hair. "What did it say?"

"'Lousy birds.'"

He laughed. He sat on the bed and put on his boots, and he shook his head and laughed again. "You really are a moron. Now come on, let's go."

"Where?" I asked.

"To the river." He picked up the gaff, put the knife in his pocket. "We have to go every day. We have to get at least a hundred fish."

"A *hundred?*" I said. "Why?"

"You want to run out of food in the middle of winter?"

He walked out of the cabin and away through the forest, leaving me staring at the open door. "What do you mean?" I shouted. But he didn't answer. I pulled on my stupid shoes and ran after him, yelling at his back, "We're not going to be here that long!"

He didn't even slow down. He just held up his hand to make a rude gesture.

"Someone will come and find us," I said. My voice was swallowed up by those huge old trees and the blankets of moss. I ran to catch up with Frank and tugged at his arm. "You don't really think we'll be here all winter, do you?"

"How should I know?" He pulled away from me. "But the salmon won't be here."

I hadn't thought of that. But Frank was right. When the last salmon in the pool had made its way over the falls, there would be no more till summer came again.

Along the cliffs, then along the beach, I trailed a few

yards behind Frank. He stopped near the *Reepicheep* to cut a coil of rope from a big snarl among the logs. He went straight to the pool and started fishing. There were even more salmon than before, their dark backs rising from the water as they swam against the current. In less than a minute Frank had one laid out on the rocks.

"Come here," said Frank. "I'll show you how to clean them."

I was happy that he talked to me, and I knelt beside him to watch how he did it. First, he slit the salmon's belly. Then he cut away the guts and the heart and the liver all at once. He tossed them into the pool, and the seagulls pounced in a shrieking mass.

Frank rinsed the whole fish in the pool, and the blood and the scales floated away through his fingers.

"Think you can do that?" he asked.

"I guess so."

We kept fishing all morning. Frank hauled in one fish after another, and soon we had seven laid out in a row. Frank guessed they weighed nearly a hundred pounds altogether. We threaded ropes through their gills and tied them in bunches, then walked back, bent like old prospectors.

When we reached the cabin Frank didn't rest. He cut every fish in half down the spine, making slabs of red flesh and shimmering skin. He hung them from the ceiling.

"How do you know how to do this?" I asked. "I guess your great *dad* taught you."

"Sure. He taught me everything," said Frank. He used bits of wire to hang the fish, threading the pieces through the scales and skin. "They'll dry hard, like candy. You don't need a fire."

That was Frank's way of saying that he had given up on building a fire. He had tried it and failed, and would never try again. But the strange thing was that he actually believed himself. In his mind, he could still build a fire if he really wanted to. It just wasn't worth the trouble.

I couldn't imagine that the salmon would dry like candy, and by the end of that day they were starting to smell. But I didn't complain, and I didn't argue. I was afraid that if I made Frank angry he would leave, that I would wake in the morning and find the cabin empty.

I slept under the table that night, as far as I could get from the door and the window. It was another restless night spent waiting for morning, with the wild singing of wolves in the distance. To see dawn come gleaming through the little cracks made me frightened instead of happy.

But the thing did not come to tap at the window again. Night after night, as I added marks to the wall, it was the *thought* of that thing that kept me awake. Waiting for it to come scratching around the cabin was nearly as bad as hearing its voice.

I kept myself busy, and I made myself useful so that Frank would stay around. I collected bottles and filled them with water at the stream. I scraped out a pit to be a bathroom, then made a toilet by bashing a hole in the seat of a plastic chair I had dragged from the beach. I even found a little box to hold our roll of toilet paper. I gathered buckets of berries: the sour salal and the hard little huckleberries.

Frank didn't thank me. He just dragged me into his schemes, his big plans that never worked out.

"We'll make an X in the clearing," he said on our third morning. "We'll make it so big they can see it from the space station."

We trudged up and down from the beach, dragging long chains of junk like old Jacob Marley's ghost. We collected everything that was red, and we laid it out in the clearing. Frank stooped down and sighted along a stick to make sure our lines were straight. But on the first windy night, our X became a scattered sprawl of plastic bits. In a little fit, Frank kicked half the stuff back into the sea, and we never rebuilt the X.

"We'll build a raft and sail away." That was his second plan, on the seventh day. He dreamed it up as the sun went down, and spent the whole night planning a great raft forty feet long. In the morning he sent me off to gather fishing floats, barrels and buckets. He took the knife and started slashing at the tangled ropes and fishing nets.

For a while, I thought it might work. We had a small forest of logs, and more rope than we needed, and no end of things that floated. But every night the tide reached higher up the beach and stole our floats. Or the waves bashed our bundles into pieces. When Frank saw a smashed barrel tumbling in the morning surf, he looked frightened. I was sure he was somehow reliving our landing in Uncle Jack's red boat. I actually saw him tremble before he noticed me watching. "What are you looking at, moron?" he said. That same day, he stopped work on the raft, and never started again.

My notches on the wall spread toward the corner. Each marked another day of fishing at the pool, of hanging salmon up to dry, of arguing with Frank. Not one day was really happy, and one of the worst of all came on the morning when I went behind the bush we called our bathroom and discovered that Frank had used the last piece of toilet paper. Not even the cardboard tube was left. Not even the plastic bag. I had to squat with a fistful of leaves, and I felt like an animal.

How we hated each other! I couldn't stand Frank's hair flicking, his pouting, his little laugh that made me feel so small. He *tried* to make me angry, refusing to talk about his life in the city or my uncle Jack. I sometimes thought he argued just to pass the time. He got mad when I made mistakes, when I put something down in the wrong place, when I didn't answer fast enough.

Sometimes he called me such awful names that I felt like crying.

Frank still had the bed and the foam pad. It was the worst bed I'd ever seen, but I could hardly stand the thought that I had to sleep beside it, on the floor. I had to look up at him, while he looked down at me, and as long as he owned the bed he was in charge. If I wanted things to change, I would have to fight him for it, and I doubted I would win. He was too big and strong.

On my half of the cabin I got the rickety table. On my half I got the fish. Another six or seven every day, they hung mostly on my side. I had to duck and weave to get around them.

The only thing we shared was the flies. They filled the cabin as thick as raindrops, from tiny whining things to giant deerflies that could take a chunk out of a person's flesh. They buzzed at my arms, at my neck and hair. I decided that flies were the most horrible things in Alaska, not counting Frank.

On our thirteenth day in the cabin, the raven came back. I was sitting at sunset on the rocky point, hoping for a ship to come along, when I heard the peculiar whistle of his wings. I turned around to see him settling at the top of the skeleton tree, above the smallest coffin. He folded his wings and made a little croaking sound that I imagined was a raven's way of saying hello.

Hunched as he was, he looked sad and lonesome,

and I wondered if he had come to visit the body of his dead friend. I remembered wandering through the cemetery after my father died, thinking that I was going to visit him there. I hoped the raven remembered his friend soaring through the sky, not hanging from a doorway wrapped in red wire.

From the top of the tree he called again, his voice now a musical note like the sound of a wooden xylophone. Of all the sounds he made, it was the most beautiful.

I wondered if he had always perched in that same tree at the setting of the sun to sing that little song. Maybe he liked to keep company with the skeletons, or to watch over the bones. But what if he came on stormy nights, when the moon shone through ragged clouds, and he roused the skeletons from their coffins? What if he assembled their bones with his black beak and drove them down from the tree to run through the forest? It was such a gruesome picture that it made me shiver, and then laugh at my own imagination. But as I looked at the raven perched above the silvery coffins, a strange little phrase popped into my head:

The black fruit of the skeleton tree.

The Mountain

Oh, I miss my raven. I would love to see him now, but there are only hours to go until we're rescued. I know *why* he has gone, but not *where*.

I'll have to leave without him; there's no choice. And one day he will come back to the cabin and find nobody here. What will he wonder? What will he do?

I don't think he will stay long in the cabin without me. He'll hunch at the top of the skeleton tree, where he can watch for people coming. Then everything will have gone full circle, and it will be as though Frank and I had never found the place. The bones will rest in their coffins, and the raven will keep his lonely lookout.

I wonder, that day, was he watching for someone when I found him at the top of the tree, with Frank sitting alone on the shore? Maybe he was waiting for the man who'd built the cabin. He might have been waiting for years.

Or maybe even then he was plotting against Frank. Maybe everything that happened was carefully planned by the raven.

• • •

As soon as Frank came out of the forest the raven stopped his musical gurgling. He flapped his wings and rose from the tree, flying off across the forest.

Frank walked straight toward me with his hands in his pockets. His boots shuffled through the yellow grass. Then he stopped and turned, and we both stared at the mountain—at *our* mountain—with its craggy peak gleaming in the sunset. Streaks of snow were red as blood.

To me it was a beautiful sight. But Frank was thinking only of practical things. "We've got to climb that mountain," he said.

"Are you kidding?" I said. "It would take forever."

"One day up, one day down," he said. "We'd have to spend the night on the summit."

"Why?"

"To see if there are lights, moron." Frank shook his head at my stupidity. "We could see everything from there. We'd know if there were people around. We'd know if this is an island or not."

I shouldn't have been surprised. Of course Frank

would want to be the king of his world, to stand at its very top, for a little while the highest thing in existence. But I couldn't imagine crawling up the rocks and over the snow. I could never sleep up there.

"Have you ever climbed mountains?" I asked.

"Sure," he said. "Me and my dad climbed lots of them."

Again I felt a little pang of jealousy. My dad had been different. "I tried it once," I said. "My dad and Uncle Jack took a bunch of Boy Scouts—"

"You were a *Boy Scout?*" said Frank.

"Just Cubs," I told him.

It hadn't lasted very long. Uncle Jack signed me up when I was nine years old, thinking I needed friends and adventure. He liked the lady that the boys called Jacala, and volunteered to lead the troop of Cubs and Scouts into the mountains past Whistler. He made it sound like such a big adventure that even my dad came along.

We trekked up beyond the tree line, to a bare slope of flat stones that slithered under our feet.

"Don't lean into the mountain," Uncle Jack told us. "Stand up straight. Keep your feet apart." Then he set off in the lead, with Jacala beside him in her little red shorts, and my father close behind, followed by the other leaders, who were followed by the Scouts, who were followed by the Cubs. And last of all, were me and Alan.

Nobody liked Alan. He was fat and clumsy, the only kid who had never earned a badge. But he was my best friend in school, and I couldn't just leave him behind on the mountain. He was afraid of heights, afraid of falling, afraid of snakes and bears and mountain lions. We had barely stepped out onto the shale before he was crying like a baby.

"I can't do this, Chris," he said. "I'm scared."

I shouted for Uncle Jack, but he didn't answer. I shouted for my dad and heard my voice echoing through the valley. It sounded high and shrill.

They just kept going. My uncle, my father and everyone else. Alan and I hadn't gone a hundred yards, and they were already just specks on that gray mountain.

Alan trembled. He leaned forward and his feet slid out from under him. He sprawled across the stones with his arms spread out, clattering down the slope in a cloud of dust. "I can't do it," he said again.

I yelled as loudly as I could—"Dad! Uncle Jack!"—and my echo yelled it over and over. But those distant figures kept moving, and soon they vanished around the corner of the mountain.

Alan was too busy crying to call for help. He could hardly move. Angry and frustrated, I screamed for my father. But no one came back to help me.

Step by step, I led Alan along. "Stand up straight," I told him a hundred times. "Don't lean into the mountain." I carried his little canvas pack. I carried the stupid hatchet that he would not leave behind. He shuffled like a person on an icy street, and when we rounded the shoulder of the mountain, everyone else was rounding the next one.

We didn't catch up until they reached the end of the shale and stopped to eat lunch on jagged rocks. Cheered by the sight, Alan barged ahead, leaving me struggling along with his hatchet and pack. So I arrived last. Everyone else fell very quiet as I came up. Uncle Jack turned around to talk to Jacala as though he hadn't seen me. My father was sitting on a stone, eating his sandwich, and he didn't even lift his head.

I wanted him to say that I had done a good deed by helping Alan, that he was proud of me for being the only one who had stayed behind. But he didn't understand. He thought *I* was the one who needed Alan's help. He was so ashamed of his crybaby son that he lost his appetite. He stuffed his half-finished sandwich into the paper bag. "Let's get going, Jack," he said.

They never knew I had helped Alan. I didn't tell them then because Uncle Jack hated boasters. And I didn't tell them later because I didn't think they'd believe me. But I promised myself that would I never cry for help again, and that I would never go back to the mountains.

A part of me wanted to tell that story to Frank. But

I was afraid he would laugh, or tease me forever. So I said I had tried climbing mountains, and I didn't like it. But he wasn't satisfied.

"You scared?" he asked.

"No," I said, though that wasn't really true.

"Then why? Huh? Why?"

He would have kept asking all night. I said, "Because it doesn't matter, that's why. If it's an island, what's the diff? We just have to wait for someone to find us."

"What if they don't?" asked Frank.

That was impossible. "They found the cabin guy, didn't they?" I said.

"Did they?"

It was so frustrating sometimes, to talk to Frank. "Is he here?" I asked.

"Is he gone?"

That seemed like such a stupid question that I didn't know what to say. I watched the last bit of sunlight vanish from the very top of the mountain, and the blackness of the world made me see that Frank had a point. I didn't *know* that the cabin guy had been rescued. He could be wandering lost in the bush, or hiding behind a tree to watch us.

Frank stretched and groaned. "Only one of us has to climb the mountain," he said. "The other should stay here and keep fishing."

I didn't like those choices. Climb a mountain by myself and spend a night on the summit? Or stay alone in the cabin with the skeletons out there? I dreaded them both.

"Maybe we'll draw straws," said Frank.

I thought he meant to do it right then. He walked away, as though to collect sticks in the forest. But like all his plans, he left this one unfinished. I fell asleep worrying about it, and I woke worrying about it again in the middle of the night. At dawn I was still trying to figure out what to do when I heard a little scratch at the window, and that awful voice came through the walls.

Lousy birds.

This time Frank heard it too. I didn't know he'd been lying awake. But the bed groaned as he sat up. "What the heck's out there?" he said.

Seeing that Frank was frightened made me even more afraid. I crawled farther from the wall, until I knocked against the table and it rattled in the dark. The scratching at the window stopped. But the voice spoke again.

I hate you.

"It's the cabin guy," said Frank. "It has to be. He's a lunatic."

But no man would have spoken like that. The words were hisses and croaks, sounds made without lips, without a tongue or teeth.

Frank got up.

"Don't go out there," I said.

But he wouldn't listen to me. He took the gaff and

went to the door. He paused for only a moment, then pushed it open and went outside. I couldn't lie alone in the cabin waiting for something to happen. I went after him, into the gray light of the forest.

Frank was standing at the window, facing the trees. The shadows of the forest seemed deep and mysterious. Anything could be hiding there.

"This is what happens," said Frank. "People go crazy if they're alone too long." He slapped the gaff into his palm and suddenly shouted, "Come on! Where are you?"

There was just a tiny sound, a tick and scratch. Not sure where it came from, we stared all around.

No one's coming.

Frank bashed at the salal bushes. I whirled around, then stumbled back, and I looked up to see the raven standing on the cabin roof. He thrust out his head and opened his beak. That croaking voice came straight from his throat. *I hate you.*

He seemed to cough the words from deep inside him, to barf them from his gaping beak. They sounded wicked and ominous.

"He can talk," said Frank.

"I think he's just making sounds," I said. "I don't think he understands the words."

Frank stared at me. "Gee, thanks, Mr. Science." Then he rolled his eyes and flicked his hair. "You see? That thing's a pest."

The raven was peering down at us, his head turned crazily sideways. It made me laugh. "You want a treat?" I asked. "Just a minute."

I went inside to get a piece of fish. Frank came in right after me. "Don't feed that thing," he said.

"Just a little bit."

"No!" he shouted. "I didn't carry those fish all the way here so you could feed them to a *bird*."

"Then I'll give him one of the ones that *I* carried," I said.

It was ridiculous. I couldn't tell one salmon from the other, and Frank knew it. But he didn't stop me as I tore a piece from the tail of a fish and went back out. I broke the flesh into pieces, which I tossed to the raven. He caught them easily in his beak and gobbled them down.

"Frank, come and look," I said. "He's done this before."

Inside, Frank peered up through the window, looking just like the bird peering down. It made me laugh again.

The raven wiped his beak on the roof, rasping it back and forth. He ruffled the feathers on his folded wings and cried out to me.

"You want more, you'll have to come down and get it," I said.

I moved a few yards from the cabin, into the ghostly edges of the morning. I knelt there and held out the fish.

It was comical how the raven fretted. He paced at the edge of the roof, then dropped to the ground and turned in little circles. He hopped toward me; he hopped away. But very slowly, an inch or two at a time, he came nearer.

It was a long time before he stood close enough that I could feed him. I held out my hand with a piece of fish in my fingers, and he leaned forward as far as he could. He leaned so far that he lost his balance and had to catch himself with frantic flaps of his wings. He was a little clown who made me laugh out loud.

He tipped his head and stared at me with one black eye as round and bright as a little marble. *You took it,* he whispered. Then he came the rest of the way in one hop and plucked the fish from my fingers. He ate it right there, watching me as he gobbled it down. I fed him another piece before I tried to touch him. He watched my hand move slowly nearer, then closed his eyes and trembled all over. But he didn't move away. With just the tips of my fingers I brushed the feathers on his wings. They were surprisingly cold and coarse. I touched his back, his shoulder, moving my fingers slowly toward the little feathers that made overlapping rows around his neck. But he'd had enough. With a cry, he opened his huge wings and flew up into the trees.

I watched him go, feeling a warm sort of wonder, a

longing to touch him again. I hoped I had not scared him away forever.

"When you've finished playing with the bird we'll go fishing," said Frank, who was still inside the cabin.

"He's already gone," I said.

"Good."

A few minutes later, we went too. The gray dawn became a beautiful morning, all bright and crisp, with the waves breaking in blue streaks.

Frank started catching fish right away, and he whistled a song. For the first time in ages I was really happy. I kept thinking of the raven and the feel of its feathers. Hoping it would come again to the tree at the edge of the river, I sat close to the falls to clean the fish.

It was a job I could do without thinking, and I quickly lost myself in the swirling water and the circling fish, in the numbing sound of the falls. It was like staring into a fire, and my thoughts were carried away. When, all at once, the gulls rose in a cloud and vanished, I barely heard the roar of their wings.

"Hey," said Frank. "Look who's here."

On the other side of the river, just a hundred yards away, a bear was plodding toward us.

"*Ursus horribilis*," said Frank in a dead sort of voice. "A grizz."

A grizzly bear, he meant. A strange smile appeared on his face as we watched the bear come nearer.

It walked like a machine, swaying from side to side, each huge foot swinging slowly forward. It moved along steadily, as though nothing could stop it.

"We should go back," I said.

"No."

Frank didn't look the least bit worried. His feet wide apart, he stood slapping the gaff against his palm, like a policeman in a riot squad.

The bear just kept coming. Every step carried it exactly the same distance in exactly the same direction, over stones and pebbles, over logs and rocks, over anything in its way.

"I bet he weighs half a ton," said Frank. "But no one in the world could outrun him. He can go thirty miles an hour."

I hadn't thought that Frank cared much about anything, but he seemed nearly awed by the bear. We could hear the clatter of stones as it walked.

"Come on, let's go," I said. But Frank wouldn't move.

"We have to stand our ground," he told me.

"What?"

"This is our territory."

"No it's not." I said.

"It is now." Frank flashed the same smile I'd seen many times on Uncle Jack. "That's how a bear thinks. This side of the river is ours, and we have to protect it."

My heart thumped in my chest, sweat trickled down my ribs, and I had a terrible sense of waiting. I could see the bear's claws flashing white; I could hear them tick against the stones. In a minute or two it would reach the pool.

But suddenly it stopped. It thrust its muzzle down among the rocks and snuffled loudly. It rolled aside an enormous rock and gobbled up the little crabs hidden underneath. Then it raised its head and sniffed. Its black nose twitched.

"He can't see very well," said Frank. "But he knows we're here. Don't move."

I hardly breathed. The bear stood up on its hind legs. It looked around; it sniffed, then dropped slowly onto all fours again and turned toward the trees. It strode up the beach and over the logs—over the logs as though they weren't there—to slip into the darkness of the forest.

For a few moments I could trace the bear's path by the breaking of branches and the swaying of big trees. Then everything seemed still and quiet.

Frank kept smiling. In some strange way, he was enjoying himself. "Okay," he said. "Let's get some fish."

"No way," I told him. "We don't know where that bear's going."

"But we know he's *gone*," said Frank. "He doesn't care about us. He'll go up the river and scoop his dinner from a shallow spot."

"How do you know that?"

"Because he's a lazy old bear," said Frank. He went

back to his fishing, crouched by the side of the pool as though nothing could scare him.

I couldn't concentrate on the salmon I was cleaning. I kept looking around, down along the beach and up toward the forest. And soon the bear appeared again.

It stepped from the bushes at the top of the falls, just a few yards from where I was cleaning the fish. "Frank," I called quietly. "It's back."

He stood up at the side of the pool, the gaff in his hand. "Stay right there," he told me.

The bear waded out into the river, right at the brink of the falls. When I looked back at Frank I was amazed to see him smiling. The closeness of the bear excited him.

At that moment he was my uncle Jack. The daredevil. I heard my mother's warning: *You have to be careful of men who love danger.*

The bear waded halfway across the river, then stepped down into the falls, to a rocky ledge where the river broke into creamy curls.

"Hold your ground," said Frank.

The bear swept its paw through the churning water. It ducked its head into the froth and came out with a salmon trapped in its jaws, an enormous fish that writhed and flapped. But the bear carried it easily, to the top of the falls and on up the river.

Frank watched it go with that expressionless look of his. He was somehow satisfied now that we had faced the bear, and he began to collect the fish that we'd caught. We carried them back to the cabin, where we split them open and hung them to dry. The cabin already seemed crowded with fish. "They're supposed to grow a crust," said Frank. He peered at one of the first fish we'd caught, then tapped it with his knuckles. A little swarm of flies rose up and buzzed around him. "I guess it hasn't happened yet."

We ate another dinner of fish and seaweed. Frank brought a handful of grass that he called sedge. It was stiff, with triangular edges, and it stuck out from each side of our mouths as we chewed, until we looked like a pair of cows. Then Frank pretended to be Snidely Whiplash, twirling a green mustache. That made me laugh, and he laughed too, until we rolled on the sand with our hands on our stomachs.

But that night I heard Frank crying. His sobbing woke me up, and I didn't move a muscle, though my hip pressed painfully on the floor. At first, I didn't want him to know I could hear him. But he must have cried for hours, smothering the sound in his mattress. The wooden bed groaned every time he shook. He sounded so sad that I became afraid.

"Frank?" I finally said, as quiet as the raven's whisper.

Instantly, his sobs turned to little gasps as he tried to control his crying.

"Are you okay?" I asked.

"Just shut up," he said.

The bed creaked as he rolled over, turning his back toward me. I heard him sniff and snuffle.

"Frank, what are you thinking about?" I asked.

He didn't answer.

"Are you thinking about your mom?" I thought often of mine. "You know what? I bet my mom knows something's wrong. She always feels it. I bet she's looking out the front window right now. That's what she does when she's scared. She stands with her arms crossed, looking out that window. Hey, Frank, what do you think *your* mom's doing?"

"Getting drunk." He made a little snorting noise. "That's what she does when she's scared. That's what she does when she's happy. That's what she does when she's sad. That's what—"

"Do you try to help her?" I asked.

"No, she gets drunk just fine on her own."

It didn't sound as though Frank spent much time thinking about his mother. I wondered if he missed his friends, and that was why he was crying. According to our wall calendar of scratches and gouges, school had started already. I imagined Frank had tons of cool friends who stood around flicking their hair. He probably had a girlfriend.

That made me think of Alan. I pictured him going alone to school. Everyone else would be running along, laughing, and Alan would puff his way along the hall looking only at the tiles on the floor, at the dangling laces of his enormous sneakers. He would feel as lonely there, in that busy place, as I felt in Alaska. *We're all of us castaways.*

Frank sniffed once more. He said, "Tell me about your dad."

"Why?" I said. "What about him?"

"I dunno," said Frank. "What was he like?"

It seemed an odd thing to ask. I doubted if Frank cared at all about my dad. He just wanted to hear me talk, to somehow fill his loneliness, the way he might have turned on a radio back home.

"When he was a kid he was really good at everything," I said. "He was in this huge spelling bee once, and he was the third-best speller in the whole country. And he played hockey. He could have been a forward in the NHL. A scout from the Oilers even came to see him, but—"

"I mean as a father," snapped Frank, interrupting. "What was he *like*? What did he do for fun?"

"Nothing," I said.

"Oh, come on!"

"Why are you so angry?" I asked. "He just didn't have fun, that's all. He never did anything." It sounded pathetic, even to me. "Except when I was little—he was happy then," I said. "We used to play games and go on treasure hunts."

"Like pirates?"

"Yes."

Frank was quiet for a while. "So what happened?"

"What do you mean?" I said.

"Moron. Why did he stop having fun?"

I ignored the insult. It took nothing to make Frank angry. "I guess he didn't have time to have fun," I said. "He was always busy. Always working. He started going away on business trips all the time. It was like he didn't want to be home anymore."

"So where did he *want* to be?"

"Just somewhere else, I guess." I hadn't really thought about that. "He didn't choose where to go; he was just *sent* places. But he never took pictures, and he never brought home souvenirs."

"Did you ever think he was like a hit man or something?" asked Frank.

I laughed. My father the hit man—it was such a crazy idea. He carried a spare tie in his briefcase, just in case he spilled something on the one that he wore. In his pocket he kept a little wad of toilet paper that he refreshed every morning, probably counting out the exact number of squares. He tried to get Mom and me to do that too. "Trust me," he told us. "You don't want to touch the paper in a public bathroom."

He had become boring, that was the thing. Old and boring.

"What about his trips?" asked Frank. "Did he have fun on his trips?"

"I don't know. Maybe," I said. "He was always happy

to go away, that's for sure. And when he came home he seemed sad."

"Oh, really?" said Frank, as though he found that interesting.

We talked until dawn. Through the boards on the window, a gray light appeared. Then the raven arrived and perched on the sill. He tapped on the plastic pane.

I wriggled out of the space blanket and stood up. "I'm going to let him in," I said.

"Don't," said Frank.

"Why not?"

"It's like Dracula."

That sounded so stupid, it made no sense. I pushed aside a slab of salmon and stared at Frank on the bed. "How's he like Dracula?"

"Don't you know anything?" said Frank. "Dracula can't go into a house until he's invited. But if you ask him in, he'll kill you."

"I'll take my chances," I said.

I grabbed a board and pulled it loose. The raven stood on the sill, a black bird shape against the plastic. I tore off the rest of the boards and spread the slit in the plastic flaps. "Come in," I said.

He hopped through the window without a care, as though he had done it a thousand times. He hopped straight down to the floor, and in his funny, lurching way explored every part of the cabin. He looked under the bed and under the table. He pecked at the things in the orange box, and especially at the shiny little whistle. "You want to play with that?" I asked.

He turned his head and blinked at me, as though he understood. When I took the whistle out of the box he twitched like a cat that had seen a mouse. He pounced on it when I put it down, and rolled it across the floor with his beak, chasing it into the corners of the room.

I laughed out loud, and the raven made little cackling sounds. But Frank didn't even smile. Into the corner, the raven chased the whistle. He batted it out with his beak and sent it rolling under the bed.

He looked up at me.

"Go on," I said. "Go get it."

But he wouldn't go under the bed. Instead, he looked at Frank, who was lying on his side on the mattress.

"Don't look at *me*," said Frank. "I'm not going to get it for you."

The raven's eyes were bright and shiny. He shook his tail and said, *Lousy birds*. And he laughed again, in his rattling way.

"He's weird," said Frank. "Don't you know it's bad luck to have a raven in the house?"

"Why?" I asked.

"It's a bad omen."

A bad omen. I laughed. Actually, I sort of giggled. And that was enough to make Frank angry again.

"They've got lice, moron. They bring diseases," he said. "Death and ravens go together, so don't laugh." He threw off his jacket and pushed his way through the drying fish, heading for the door.

The raven fluttered quickly out of his way, up to the chair, up to the window. He perched there, panting, until the door closed behind Frank. Then he came down again and stood right beside me.

• • •

I was not used to having a pet. Every year, at Christmas and my birthday, I'd asked for a dog, and once for a snake because I thought the kids might like me if I showed up at school with a python around my neck. But Dad didn't care for dogs, and Mom despised reptiles in general. Then Dad broke down and got me a hamster. But it lived for less than a month. When the raven came into the cabin and chose *me* for his friend, it was as though my birthday wishes had suddenly come true. For three mornings in a row he pushed through the cabin window, and each day he stayed a little longer. But he was always gone before dark.

He was a funny, clever thing, and I thought I would never get tired of watching him. He invented little games, sometimes clinging by his beak to a slab of fish while I pushed him like a kid on a swing. When I laughed, his eyes took on a special twinkle. It pleased him to make me happy.

But I was always startled to hear him speak. *I hate*

you, he'd say. *Lousy birds.* His voice was eerie and ominous, and it made my skin crawl.

"Can't you teach that thing new words?" asked Frank. But if I had somehow taught the raven to recite Shakespeare, Frank would not have been satisfied. He told me over and over, "I hate that bird." Or, "I don't want that bird coming anywhere near me," as though there was any fear of *that.* The raven wanted only to be with me.

Maybe Frank was jealous. I doubted he had ever been the kid picked last for baseball games, the one left without a partner for a classroom project. But whenever I began to feel sorry for him, he found a way to change my mind.

"You know that bird will fly away when winter comes," he told me as I sat feeding the raven. "It doesn't care about you; it's only hanging around 'cause you feed it."

"Sure," I said.

"It's like the bear. It thinks only about eating, sleeping and surviving. If you stopped feeding it, I bet it would peck your eyes out."

"Sure," I said again.

"Just wait and see." Frank went away in a huff. The raven watched him go, then tipped his head and gazed at me. *Hate that bird,* he said very clearly.

That evening I counted the marks I had made on the wall, realized with a fright that nearly three weeks had passed and tried to figure out what day it was. My poor dead watch didn't even have a calendar. So I asked Frank.

"It's Sunday," he told me.

Of course he didn't know; he just made it up. But Sunday was as good a day as any, and I counted back from there to the day I'd found my raven in the bushes. Thinking like Robinson Crusoe, I named him Thursday.

He liked to perch on my shoulder, like a pirate's black parrot. Sometimes he faced forward, and sometimes backward, and he pulled at my hair with his beak, or nibbled gently at my ear, though that always made me squirm and laugh. Frank watched, smoldering with jealousy.

On our twenty-second day the wind shifted to the south and rose to a gale. Enormous waves thundered on the rocks. Rain pelted through the forest with machine-gun sounds, and the trees swayed and creaked around us. It was the first real sign of winter coming, a hint of what the months ahead would bring. West Coast weather was always predictable. Once the winds shifted to the south, storm would follow storm, and the sun would disappear. Rain would only end when it turned to snow instead.

Thursday kept close beside me. As the wind gusted he whistled low notes that sounded like wailing creatures.

"He's evil," said Frank.

"Well, I like him," I said. I drew Thursday up onto

my lap and tickled the feathers on his belly. "Didn't you ever have a dog or anything?"

"I did when I was little," said Frank. He was lying on his back on the bed. "All I remember is that he was a really old dog, and his name was Ghost."

"That's weird," I said.

"Why?"

"I had a hamster called Ghost."

"That *is* weird," said Frank. The wind gusted, and the raven whistled.

"It was Dad's idea," I said. "I wanted to call him Sleepy because he slept all day. I never saw him except at night. Then Dad said, 'Call him Ghost.'"

Frank smiled at my little story. "You should have called the raven Ghost. He's spooky."

I leaned back. Thursday hopped up to my shoulder and rubbed his beak against my lips. I opened my mouth and let him peck the tiny shreds of salmon between my teeth. Frank groaned, but he grinned as well. "That's disgusting."

I laughed. "Yeah, it is." Then I opened my mouth a little wider, and Thursday tilted his black head to reach right in.

Frank covered his eyes and turned away. But now he was laughing too, and in our tiny cabin that shook in the storm, I was happy. I couldn't remember the last time I had sat with someone and talked about simple things. Mrs. Lowe's nagging comment—*Christopher has trouble making friends*—was still true. But at least I *had* made a friend. I had nearly made two.

"It drives me crazy sitting in here," said Frank. He sat up and scratched his head. "Let's go out."

It was raining bullets. We hauled out the plastic sheets the cabin guy had saved and turned them into capes and leggings. They were so ragged that we had to wear three at the same time. When we opened the door the wind tore it away, slamming it back against the wall. That was too much for Thursday. He peered out at the rain and wouldn't go past the door. Like a pair of giant birds ourselves, with enormous, flapping wings, Frank and I went down to the sandy beach.

Masses of things had come ashore. There were dozens of bottles and chunks of foam, scraps of wood and plastic. There were things that were sad and poignant too: a stroller with three wheels; a plastic doll in a white dress that rolled in the surf like a drowned child. I found a torn blanket I could wear as a poncho, and that pleased me. But we didn't stay very long on the beach.

"This is crazy," said Frank. The wind shredded his plastic clothes. The rain made him squint and frown. "Let's go back."

We trekked back to the cabin, past trees that swayed like grass. And we found the raven stealing our food.

Standing on the table, pecking at a fish, he looked like a boxer with a punching bag. As he jabbed with his beak, the slab of fish whirled away on the rope. He hopped back and forth. He ducked his head; he lunged and pecked again. Bits of flesh fell from the fish, covering the table in specks of pink and red.

Pucka-pucka-pucka. Thursday's black beak punched at the fish. The rickety table squeaked and squealed underneath him, and the fish swung in and out.

For a moment Frank just stood in the doorway, watching. Then he ran into the cabin and snatched up the gaff.

Maggots

A sound like a gunshot startles me out of my memories. It's loud and flat, and I look up with the thought that someone has fired a signal.

But the sea is empty. I realize that all I heard was the slap of a seal's tail, or the burst of a whale's breath.

In the north, the fogbank looks bigger. The sun glares off the top of it, but underneath it's thick with shadows. I wonder if the ship that will save us is traveling along inside it, ready to burst at any moment into the sunshine.

Today is the day we'll be saved. I believe that. Maybe when I reach the end of the novel, when Kaetil finds the man who killed his father, that's when they'll arrive. I convince myself it's true—until I remember that there *is* no ending. Not anymore.

I take the book from the bucket and bend it open. A page falls out, fluttering away like an autumn leaf. It will leave another small hole in the story, something for Frank to argue about.

I find my place near the beginning. The Skraelings have murdered Valgaard on his farm, and now the man with yellow eyes is running across the fields, chasing Valgaard's wife and child.

Over the meadow she ran, over the stony slope. On her back bounced Kaetil, laughing at the game. But this was no game. The man with yellow eyes chased them to the river, where the woman dropped to her knees, down to her knees she fell, and with her arms shielded little Kaetil.

"Please," she begged. "Please spare the boy. Oh please."

But her pleas fell on deaf ears. With one blow the Skraeling split her skull. Kaetil lay beside her, giggling at the sight of his toes sticking up in the air. He tried to touch them and giggled again. The man with yellow eyes washed his sword in the river and left them lying together in the grass.

At dusk, the ravens came.

I don't understand why Frank loves this book so much. To me, the best parts are the notes that the cabin guy made. They're scrawled with a red felt pen. *True! Ravens flocked to battlefields.* All through the book are similar comments. In his lonely cabin, the man must have become obsessed with the story. He knew a lot about ravens.

I keep thinking of Thursday.

• • •

When Frank barged into the cabin, Thursday lifted his head. In the raven's eyes was a look of fear and betrayal, and he shrieked as he spread his wings. Frank swung the gaff.

"Don't!" I shouted.

There was an awful thud. Frank had missed Thursday and hit the swinging slab of fish instead. It exploded into chunks of flesh and bone.

"Stop it!" I cried.

But Frank was in a fury, and the raven in a panic. They blundered around the cabin, through the dangling fish. Thursday smashed against the window, screaming in fright. He tried to squirm out through the hole, then fled across the cabin and up toward the smoke hole. Frank stumbled over the wooden chair and hurled it out of his way.

"Frank, stop!" I shouted. "Leave him alone."

Thursday was flapping so hard against the roof that I thought he would break his wings. Frank smashed another salmon, splattering the wall with bits of bone. Thursday took his chance to fly out through the open door.

"I'll kill him!" cried Frank. "I swear to God I'll kill him."

We stood at the table, both breathing heavily as we looked at the destruction around us. A dozen salmon—a week's worth of food—lay smashed into ragged chunks all over the cabin. Nearly bare skeletons hung from the ceiling, still swinging and turning on their hangers.

It was such an awful waste. And to make it even worse, Thursday had eaten only a tiny bit of fish, if anything at all. The table was covered with little bits of flesh, as though he had pecked the fish apart just for the pleasure of destroying it.

I felt sad and hopeless. And then I saw the maggots.

They crawled in and out of the pieces of salmon. They writhed on the floor and squirmed on the table-top. It wasn't the salmon the raven had been after. It was the maggots.

I grabbed one of the hanging fish and twisted it like a rope. A clump of maggots tumbled out. I saw others twitching among the ribs and the backbone.

It was the same for the next fish and the one after that. It was the same for nearly every salmon that we'd caught. The sight made me sick. I had eaten that fish—we had both eaten it—just the night before.

We threw away every salmon that we'd caught, hauling them down the trail. From the top of the skeleton tree, Thursday watched us drag the salmon to the rocks. Black and ragged-looking, he stood in silence.

"He doesn't understand why we're throwing out the fish just when it's getting ripe," I said, trying to make Frank smile. I held up a piece of maggoty fish and called Thursday down to get it. But the raven wouldn't move from the tree.

"He looks sad," I told Frank. "You should tell him you're sorry."

"I'm not telling him I'm *sorry*," said Frank. "He was stealing the fish."

"He was stealing the *maggots*."

"Well, I'm still not saying I'm sorry," said Frank with a flick of his hair. "He should say sorry to me." Then he started laughing—and so did I—because it seemed so stupid. And Thursday, up in the tree, made one of his lovely raven sounds, as though it pleased him to see us happy.

Piece by piece, we threw every fish we'd caught into the sea. Frank stared down at the little stains of salmon oil that bubbled up to the surface. He brushed crumbs of salmon from his hands. "We have to start all over," he said. "But we've got to have a fire. We *have* to have a fire."

"How?" I asked.

"I don't know." He crossed his arms. "Oh, I wish my dad was here."

He had never sounded so small. He was, for a moment, a little boy convinced that everything would be all right if only his dad could appear. I remembered thinking like that when I was little, believing my father was a superman, stronger and smarter than anyone in the world. I couldn't remember when that had changed.

We tried everything we could think of to start a fire. We chipped stones against other stones, and stones against metal, trying to make a spark. We gathered bits of glass from old bottles and shattered fishing floats and tried to focus sunlight onto little piles of moss and twigs.

But nothing worked, and that night we went to bed hungry for the first time in many days. Frank jammed bits of wood in the window frame, and when Thursday came to the cabin in the morning, he *ordered* me not to let him in. I didn't want to get into a big fight, so I just covered my ears as the raven tapped and muttered. It was hours before he gave up and went away.

We had no breakfast. Dead flies and flakes of salmon lay all over the floor. I brushed the mess away as Frank settled down to try to make fire again. With a bunch of sticks, and an awful sigh of resignation, he went to work. "I saw this on *Survivorman,*" he said. "It can't be that hard."

I didn't want to sit there and watch him get angry, so I went walking along the beach to look for cigarette lighters. Wrapped up in my poncho blanket, I thought I looked like Zorro.

Thursday appeared as soon as I reached the sand,

but he stayed in the treetops, dashing from one to another in funny little bursts of fancy flying. He flipped on his back or rolled right over, as he zoomed from tree to tree. I searched through the driftwood, peering under every log. When I found a lighter I snatched it up with a shout. But it was rusted and useless.

Thursday came down to see what I was doing. He followed me along the logs, peering into the places I searched. Then he strutted along ahead of me, bouncing from log to log. It surprised me when he plucked a lighter from a tangle of wood. It amazed me when he did it again. He laid them out on the sand and called to me with a little cry. "You're a clever bird," I said, and he answered with a funny chirping sound.

When I climbed the trail back to the cabin, Thursday was again riding on my shoulder. I had three lighters in my pocket, and a plan to light the gas inside them, and I felt like a Stone Age hunter bringing fire to his cave. I could hardly wait to show Frank.

But he wasn't there.

Our bits of glass were scattered across the floor. So were two of Frank's sticks, snapped angrily in half and tossed away. A third was stuck like a knife into the foam mattress. I felt a bit sorry for Frank.

I sat and watched Thursday playing with the glass. He had arranged six pieces near the stones of the fire circle, and now he stood perfectly still beside them.

When a beam of sunlight burst through the window and sparkled on the glass, he rushed forward and shuffled the pieces around. He moved them here; he moved them there; he turned them with his beak and talons. Then he stepped back and bobbed his black head, as though to see how they shone.

The beam of light vanished, and the cabin darkened, and Thursday didn't move until another shaft of light set his pieces glowing. Again, he moved them around in a great hurry.

I watched him do this four times before I realized it was more than a game. He was using the glass for prisms, shining sunlight into the dark space below the bed. At last, with a sharp cry, he darted under there and came back holding something in his beak. He set it down in front of me. The knob from the radio.

I put it on the narrow windowsill and reached out to pet Thursday. He nuzzled against me. *Clever bird,* he said.

"Yes," I told him. "You're a very clever bird." He hopped up onto my lap. I stroked the little feathers on the top of his head, feeling the hardness of his skull underneath.

"Where's Frank?" I asked. Thursday peered at me as though he knew but just couldn't say.

It was late in the afternoon when I walked to the stream in the forest, and on to the very high cliffs. I looked north toward the river, but saw no sign of Frank.

Of course I imagined all sorts of things: that he had gone at last to climb his mountain; that he had fallen from the rocks into the sea; that the bear or a wolf had caught him. And then a thought even worse came into my mind: that someone had come to save him. Maybe a boat had gone by, or a helicopter had landed, and Frank was on his way home. I could imagine him sitting with his rescuers, not saying a thing about me, just watching with that smug look as the land faded in the distance. If anyone could do that, it was Frank.

The sun began to set and there was still no sign of him. I picked a few handfuls of berries and sedge, and went back to the cabin. It felt lonely and deserted. The empty bed seemed sad, with the shape of Frank pressed vaguely into the foam.

On my shoulder, Thursday looked around. *Filthy birds*, he muttered.

Even then I didn't sit on the bed. I folded up in my own little place on the floor, and it was quite a long time before I suddenly noticed that the gaff was missing. "He went fishing!" I shouted, slapping my hand against my forehead. That startled Thursday and I laughed, relieved.

"I'm so stupid," I said. I should have thought of looking for the gaff. If I'd noticed sooner I could have gone up to the river. But now it was too late, too dark. I could only sit and wait for Frank to come back.

When the sun set, Thursday flew away. I tried hard

to keep him inside, but he went out through the window, into the darkness. I peered after him until he vanished, wondering where it was that he went every night. As the sound of his wings faded, my worst nightmare came true. I was alone in the wilderness.

I couldn't stop thinking of the hugeness of Alaska, of the mountains and snow, of the forests full of bears and wolves. I thought of the cabin guy. The skeletons. I wanted to cry, to scream for help, just as I had imagined on the airplane.

I closed myself up in the cabin and took the cigarette lighters from my pocket. In the last bit of daylight I tried desperately to make a fire.

On the beach it had seemed easy. I had imagined every step: how I'd twist the metal tops; how I'd pry the little flints. The gas wasn't important; we had the can of fuel from the cabin guy's stove. All I needed was a spark.

But the metal wouldn't bend as I wanted. The flints were ground away, or frozen by rust, and I threw everything away in frustration. I heard one lighter ricochet off the wall, another rattle on the floor, and I shouted, "Stupid useless lighters!" I heard my voice—shrill as the one on the mountain—and felt ashamed. I was acting just like Frank. Maybe we were not so different after all.

Lonely and frightened, I hugged myself in the darkness.

I rocked like a baby. And finally I broke the promise

I'd made on the mountain and cried for my father to help me.

When the window began to brighten, I thought morning had arrived. But it was only the moon rising over the distant mountains, filling the cabin with a cold and silvery light. All the things blinded by the dark began to move outside. Something scurried past the door. Something chattered; something screamed. Then something big came tramping along the trail, pushing through the bushes. And through the wall came the faint sound of someone whistling.

An old, forgotten memory slowly woke inside my head. The whistled notes faltered and started again. I didn't know the words, and I couldn't name the song, but I remembered where I'd heard it. I was suddenly a tiny boy again, squatting on the kitchen floor. I saw my father all scrunched up under the kitchen sink, trying to work on plumbing pipes that were, to him, as mysterious as ancient writing. He frowned and squinted, jiggled the pipes, and hummed that song.

He had come to save me! With the memory so strong in my mind, my first thought was to rush out to meet him, my big, towering father, who would sweep me up in his arms. But he was dead. For a year he'd been lying in his grave, and he couldn't possibly be out there in the forest.

The little snatch of song came whistled again. A cold prickle tingled down my neck at the thought of my dead father out there. Had I wished him alive, back from the grave?

I had seen his ghost before.

On the night before his funeral, as I had lain in bed remembering things good and bad, he had appeared in my doorway and waved to me sadly. Just for a moment he'd been there. But a year before that, on a drizzly Sunday in Vancouver, I had seen something even more puzzling.

Dad was in Chicago on a business trip, two thousand miles away. He had been gone three days and wouldn't be home for three days more. I wasn't even thinking about him as I rode the SkyTrain with Mom. I looked down as the train squealed around the bend to the Dunsmuir Tunnel, and there he was at a traffic light, stepping out into the street. I saw him for less than a second, in a *clack-click-clack* of the train wheels, striding over the white lines on the crosswalk. His legs, and the shadows of his legs, worked like scissors, everything shiny in the rain. "There's Dad!" I shouted. "Don't be silly," said Mom, turning in her seat. Then the tunnel closed around us.

I wanted to get off at the next station, to go back and find him. But Mom said no. "Your father's in Chicago; you know that. It was just someone who looked like your dad." But I knew what I'd seen, and I made her call him on the cell phone. "Oh, for heaven's sake," she said. But she fished it out of her purse and called, and

I heard his voice telling her the exact same thing. "I'm in Chicago; you know that." But she looked so worried and pale that I thought she believed I had seen his doppelgänger, or a changeling or something.

The feeling that had come over me then returned as I crouched in the corner of the moonlit cabin. I heard the door rattle. Then it opened. A figure stood in the moonlight, and a creaky voice spoke to me.

"Greetings, earthlings."

I gasped. But it was only Frank who stood there, only Frank who laughed at my fear. For once he was happy. "I got a fish," he said, holding it out.

It was a small one, and he had eaten more than half of it. He tossed me the rest, then put the gaff on the table. "I got caught by the tide on the way back," he said. "I had to wait at that old wreck. But look what I found."

From his jacket pocket he produced something dark and shiny. But it was his hand that I stared at: his right hand, as white and puffy as a marshmallow.

"What's wrong with your hand?" I said.

He only glanced at it. "That's salmon slime," he said. "It's nothing."

"But you're swollen up," I said.

He was shouting now. "That's just the slime! It gets in your cuts. I told you, it's nothing." He slammed onto the table the thing that he'd brought from the beach.

It was a purse. A little pink purse made of shiny plastic, it was a thing a child must have carried.

"What's inside it?" I asked.

"I don't know," he said. "It's rusted shut."

Frank was pouting. He was angry that I'd been more interested in his swollen hand than in the purse that he'd found. It sat between us now, its little brass catch turned brown with rust.

He could have opened that lock in a moment. I realized that he had wanted to wait until he was with me, to share the excitement of looking inside it. Now he just sighed, sniffed and whistled once more those few little notes.

"What's that song?" I asked.

He growled at me. "I don't know. It came into my head and I can't get it out. My mom used to sing it."

In a moment he was asleep. His legs were still bent over the edge of the bed, and he was lying in the exact same position in the morning, when Thursday woke him with a raven call.

The bird's head appeared in the window. His little eye swiveled toward me, but he wouldn't come in.

"What's wrong with it now?" asked Frank.

"I think he's scared of you," I said.

"Good."

I had to get up and stand guard by the window while Thursday slipped into the cabin. He hopped up to my shoulder and down to the table, where the child's pink purse lay still unopened. Thursday nudged it with his beak. He was always attracted to things that sparkled.

"Give me that," said Frank. "I'll open it."

He struggled to sit up. His legs had gone stiff, and he lurched across the cabin like a robot. From his pocket he took out my knife, then pried at the latch. With a little crackling sound, it broke loose and flicked away across the cabin.

Frank emptied the purse onto the bed, just as he had shaken out the orange box on our first day in the cabin. On the table, Thursday leaned forward to watch, his black eyes shining. I stood beside Frank as he sorted quickly through the things.

He sounded disappointed. "Look at that," he said. "What a stupid bunch of junk."

But it wasn't stupid, and it wasn't junk. The whole life of a little girl lay scattered across the bed. There was a small stuffed cat and a yellow paper clip, a little toy horse with blue eyes, a silver tiara made of plastic. A blue sucker had turned to a sticky mess, and four tiny worry dolls made of thread and cloth were tangled together, their arms entwined as though they were hugging each other.

There were other things too. None was any use to us, but to one little girl in Japan they must have been the most important things in the world. It seemed awful that they were disconnected now—and forever—from the memories that had made them valuable. Without those connections, maybe they were only junk. It made me remember when my father died and I kept finding his things where he'd left them: his cuff links and tie clasps, the crumpled wrapper from a candy bar. When I went into the garage a month later, I found a coffee mug balanced on the seat of my old bicycle, and it still had coffee in it.

But Frank couldn't see past the junk. "I can't believe I wasted my time with *that!*" he shouted. He scattered the little girl's treasures across the mattress. He hurled the purse against the wall. "It's junk."

"What did you expect?" I asked.

"Something good. I don't know: maybe a magnifying glass or a lighter that actually works. Maybe a cell phone. Who knows?"

A cell phone. So that was what Frank had *really* been hoping for. That was why he had waited to open the purse—so I could be there as he pulled out the cell phone and dialed 911. *Oh, hi, this is Frank....* The thought made me feel sorry for him.

"A cell phone wouldn't be any good anyway," I said. "It would be all wet and—"

"It would still have a battery, moron," said Frank.

"So what?"

He glared at me. "You think you're so smart? Figure it out."

I could think of only one thing. "You mean the cabin guy's radio?"

It still sat on the shelf above the bed. Frank even glanced toward it. "Those batteries can last forever if they're charged." He sounded angry, as though he thought I wouldn't believe him. But he was frustrated that his plan had not worked out.

"I never knew girls carried so much stupid stuff," he said. Then he grabbed the corner of the mattress and dumped everything onto the floor.

Without a word, I dropped to my knees and picked it all up. Thursday, thinking it was just a game, rounded up the little horse and the worry dolls. I packed the things carefully into the purse again, knowing I was doing exactly what some little girl must have done in Japan on the morning of the tsunami. Of course Frank laughed at me. "Playing dollies?" he asked.

He flicked his hair. It was a filthy clump that hung over his eyes now, matted with salt and tree sap. "Give me that," he said, holding out his hand. "I'll throw it away."

"No," I said.

"Why not?"

I didn't want to tell him what I had in mind. He wouldn't understand; he would say it was stupid. He stood with his hand reaching out, but I wouldn't give him the purse.

That made him angry again. He grabbed my wrist; he grabbed the purse. He tried to twist it out of my hands, but I turned away and tightened my arms around it. "Leave me alone," I said.

"No!" he shouted. "Give me that."

Frank hauled me to my feet. As we reeled across the cabin, Thursday spread his wings. His beak opened wide and his eyes shone darkly.

I wrestled with Frank for the purse. He kept pulling and pushing until he drove me up against the wall. My shoulders slammed into the wood. I grunted.

With a shriek, the raven rose from the floor. His wings seemed to fill the whole cabin, and the sound they made was like wind in the forest. He swooped at Frank's head, beating it with his wings.

Frank stumbled away, his arms flailing, but Thursday swooped again.

"Stop it!" I shouted at both of them, worried at first for Thursday, and then for Frank.

My raven was trying to tear out his eyes.

Frank covered his head with his arms. The raven clutched on to him, still screaming, wings flapping. "Get him off!" shouted Frank. "Get him off!" He spun around the cabin as though he was on fire. He crashed into the table, toppling the rickety chair.

I heard the *tap! tap!* of the raven pecking at his hands. Frank kept shouting. He tried to push the bird away as he staggered across the room. Then he tripped over the firestones and dropped to his knees.

I grabbed Thursday. I put my hands around his body, closing his wings. Through the tips of my fingers I could feel his heart beating like crazy. I tried to pull him away, but his talons were locked onto Frank's skin. He was so frantic that he turned his head and tried to peck me. But I held him more tightly, and the pressure of my hands seemed to calm him. He stopped struggling and let go of Frank. As soon as I loosened my hold he burst free. He hurled himself up against the window and burst out through the flap.

Frank staggered back against the bed. He fell onto the foam pad and crashed against the wall. His hands were cut across the knuckles, scratched all the way from fingers to wrists. The right hand was worse, the one swollen by little cuts and salmon slime. With a grimace, Frank jammed it under his arm.

"Get rid of that bird or I'll kill it," he said.

"He was trying to help me," I said. "You shouldn't have pushed me like that."

In a moment, we were shouting at each other. "I told you," said Frank. "He's too wild. He's dangerous."

"He's just a raven!" I said.

I felt Frank might hit me. But he only sat on the bed, hunched up like a child. "Get out of here," he said. "Leave me alone."

I thought he was crying. "Frank—" I said.

"Leave me alone!" he screamed.

I might have yelled right back, except I realized that Frank wasn't angry at *me*. He was angry at the child for not carrying a cell phone in her purse, at the flies and the maggots for spoiling the fish, at my uncle Jack for taking us sailing. I remembered what he'd said about people going crazy, and I thought he was coming close to that himself. I quietly took the child's purse and went out to the forest.

• • •

I knew just where to go: to that quiet old forest where the moss was thick and woolly, as soft as whipped cream. I scooped out a hole. But before I laid the purse in it, I took out the four worry dolls and held them in my fist. They were too small to have hands or faces, but somehow they looked wise and somber. My mother had given me three worry dolls after my father's funeral. "Whisper to them," she'd told me. "Tell them what scares you, then put them away. They'll take on your fears and your worries so you won't have to think about them anymore." I had stayed awake all night, telling them everything, whispering my fears of my mother dying next, of being left poor and homeless. And now, in the forest of Alaska, it surprised me to see that my fears hadn't changed. I was afraid of being alone, of being hungry and cold. I held the worry dolls close to my lips and whispered these things.

As though bringing an answer, Thursday arrived. I saw him falling, wings spread, through the bolts of sunlight to land on the moss nearby. He sang with a quavering call as I put the dolls in the purse, and the purse in the ground.

He was the witness to a funeral for a girl I'd never met. Grim and black, he sat there until I finished. Then he came with me to the cabin, swooping ahead around the bends in the trail. When I opened the door he hopped right in.

I was surprised to see Frank reading *Kaetil the Raven Hunter,* and especially surprised that he seemed to be halfway through it already. I would never have imagined him with a book in his hands, and I told myself that he must have begun in the middle, or was just reading little pieces here and there. Lying flat on the bed, he glared at Thursday, who shouted a warning as he crossed the cabin and settled in the corner. They eyed each other across the small room like a pair of crazy old gold miners.

"I warned you," said Frank. "Keep that bird away from me."

"Don't worry," I said.

From my place on the floor, I watched Frank turning the pages of the book. His right hand was cut and bleeding, with a little trickle of red running toward his wrist. In our anger and our silence, I was almost happy that Thursday had hurt him. But I felt guilty when Frank tried to be pleasant.

"Listen to this," he said. He lifted the book and read aloud.

> *Kaetil swung his silver sword. Forged from fire, a wizard's gift, it shone like the flames of hell. Through the air his sword flashed, and it sang a song of death and vengeance. Like a Valkyrie it sang.*

Frank looked up at me again. "I love this story."

"What's a Valkyrie?" I asked.

He rolled his eyes. "A lady of the warlord, you moron."

10

The Old Road

The sound comes again, that flat bark like a shot. This time, when I look up, I see a tiny cloud of mist hovering over the sea. A whale is passing.

In my hands, *Kaetil the Raven Hunter* is open to the same page that Frank read aloud in the cabin. I remember being surprised—even annoyed—that he knew about Valkyries and warlords. I didn't like to think that he was smarter than me.

But now the mystery is solved.

In his hunt for the man with yellow eyes, Kaetil has come across a group of Skraelings camped by a fjord. In a fury, he slaughters them all.

> *Through the air his sword flashed and whistled, and it sang a song of death and vengeance. It sang*

like a Valkyrie, one of those beautiful ladies of the warlord.

It makes me laugh to read this. That's so like Frank to pretend to know something he'd only just learned. It seemed in those early days that he was always competing with me, as though he had to prove to himself—over and over—that he was stronger, smarter, better in every way.

But when he read, his lips moved and I could hear him, just a little. I saw it as he lay on the bed with the tattered old novel. Expressions appeared on his face for the first time. He smiled; he frowned; he looked proud and disappointed. I decided he was reading aloud so that he could *hear* the story, the way the words connected.

• • •

"Hey, Frank," I said. "When you were little, did your dad read you bedtime stories?"

He didn't look away from the book. "Why do you want to know?"

"Just wondering," I said.

"I don't remember." He looked at his hand, at the long scratches the raven had made on his knuckles. Then he turned a page and started reading again.

I grew annoyed as I watched him. "Why can't you just tell me?" I said at last. "Yes or no?"

He sighed loudly. "Look, moron, I don't remember."

"Oh, come on," I said. "How can you forget?"

He turned to me, dark with anger. "Because I can hardly remember that time at all. I can barely remember my dad back then. But my mom says he did. She says he read to me every night, sometimes for hours. Okay?"

"Okay." I shrugged. "Sorry I asked."

But that wasn't the end of it. Frank stared at the ceiling for a minute or two, tried to read for another and then started talking again. "She would hear him downstairs. He would use different voices for the people in the story, and if they were shouting he'd be shouting too. She says it was like listening to a play."

That was the most Frank had ever told me about himself. He closed his eyes and let the book fall forward on his chest, his hands folded on top of it. That pose, that peaceful expression, reminded me of my father in his coffin.

"Sometimes I think I can *almost* remember," he said. "I was maybe two years old. But I can sort of hear his voice. I wish I knew what stories he read."

"What about when you were older?" I asked. "Did he—"

"No." Abruptly, Frank opened the book again. "He found other things to do."

He sounded bitter about that. He could have asked about *my* dad, and what sort of things I had done when

I was small. But he just held up the book and blocked me out. I sat, patting the raven. The sound of Frank reading to himself was faint and whispery.

That night ended our first month in Alaska. When Thursday flew out through the window I made the thirtieth mark on the wall. I dreamed again of zombies.

They chased me through the same drowned city, through black water and neon lights. But now Uncle Jack was in the dream too, staggering among the zombies in sodden clothes covered with seaweed. He chased me with his arms reaching out, up stairways and over rooftops. No matter how fast I ran, I couldn't leave him behind. When I woke early in the morning I was out of breath.

It was a cold and rainy day. Frank was already awake, but sitting glumly by the door. Water had worked through the sheets of plastic on the roof and was dripping onto the bed. Frank just sat there, shivering, watching the drops grow on the ceiling like tiny, shivery wasp nests.

"I'm not going fishing today," he said.

"Okay," I told him. "We can fix—"

"But you can go alone." He glowered up at me. "Unless you're scared."

Well, how could I *not* go then? I put on capes and leggings and a hood, took the gaff from the table. For the first time, I got to carry the knife. I was a bit nervous about the bear, but proud to be going alone.

Down on the beach the waves were huge, rolling up beside me in big green curls. They roared and leapt along the stones, and fingers of surf reached right to the stranded logs.

There was no sign of Thursday. On windy days he sometimes played his raven games, flinging himself through the air, or clinging for as long as he could to the tips of wildly tossing trees, until the wind sent him spinning away. But on this day he had something else to do, his own wild ways to follow.

I saw an old refrigerator wallowing in the breakers, and a propane tank slamming on the stones with a sound like a gong. Spray pattered on my capes, but inside them I was dry right down to my feet. I saw myself as Robinson Crusoe in an age of plastic, in shoes that didn't match, with a belt made of rubber hose, a cone-shaped hood tied with a bit of old rope.

As soon as I reached the river, my heart began to fall. There were no seagulls squabbling over scraps, and there were very few salmon left in the pool. They swam lazily out in the middle, barely moving their fins and tails, just drifting with the current. They reminded me of the sad old people I'd seen shuffling along on the sidewalks in Vancouver. I crouched at the edge and fished a long time, but the only one that I gaffed was barely alive.

I saw a salmon tumble backward over the falls and sink into the pool. Then up it rose like a white ghost, its fins and tail nearly rotted away, and started swimming again toward the falls.

I had to follow it. If I was going to find any fish worth eating, I would have to go up the river, into the territory of the grizzly bear.

It was not an easy thing to do, and I stood for a long time at the foot of the falls, until I knew that if I waited another minute I would never go. Then I went quickly, as fast as I could, hauling myself up rocks at the very edge of the river.

At the top I found an old, forgotten road.

Only four or five feet wide, it pushed straight through the bushes. Hollowed into the ground were enormous potholes, one after the other, stretching away into the dark of the forest. They had filled with old leaves and fir needles. I wondered where the road would take me if I followed it all the way.

The roar of the falls faded behind me as I walked toward the mountain. The river became a quiet, burbling stream split into three channels that flowed over gravel and sand. It teemed with birds. Gulls crowded so closely together that I could hardly see the water in places.

I waded right into the stream. The water was painfully cold, and clear as glass, and I could see my feet in their stupid sandals, swollen by refraction until they looked like big white sausages.

All around, salmon were struggling upstream where the water was so shallow they couldn't even swim. They crawled across the gravel with their backs above the surface, their fins so worn away that they looked like Japanese fans, as thin as paper. They thrashed forward in bursts, then stopped to rest as the current pushed them back again. Along the banks lay dead ones by the hundreds.

All I had to do was bend down and hook the fish. I looked for those with the fewest wounds and scars and, afraid the bear would come along, I chose two very quickly. I cleaned them on the riverbank, ripping out skeins of scarlet eggs that I tossed among the gulls. My hands trembled as I worked. I wanted to get off the river as soon as I could, but the salmon would be lighter and easy to carry once they were gutted. When something swooped above me I got an awful fright. But it was only Thursday, arriving in a whirl of feathers and wings, with his cry of greeting. He landed beside me, and the gulls gave him room. I tossed him the guts of my second fish, and I carried him back down the river on my shoulder. I liked the press of his talons. I remembered my father reaching down to steady me when I was a little kid, his fingers squeezing in that same way.

Where the river was shaded by trees, I saw my reflection. It was twisted by the ripples and currents, but I was still shocked by the sight. A boy in plastic rags with a raven on his shoulder, two enormous salmon hanging from his hands. To me, I looked heroic.

I decided that this was how I wanted to go home. I imagined TV cameras crowding forward as I stepped out of a helicopter—straight from the Alaskan wilderness— my capes fluttering, my dark raven turning his head. I saw my mother crying, the mayor stepping out to greet me.

All the way to the cabin I thought about this: about getting home, of the things I would do and the food I would eat. I wondered if everything would seem different. I wondered if I would miss Alaska in any way. I actually wondered if I would miss Frank.

Near the end of the beach I found a roll of orange tape. It had CAUTION written on it, again and again. CAUTION, CAUTION, CAUTION for yard after yard. Thursday played a game of chasing its fluttery end as I walked. But he left me at the edge of the old forest, suddenly flying away without any sort of cry. His wing brushed my face as he flew past. Alone, I went on to the cabin, where I found new sheets of plastic stretched across the roof, weighted down with rocks and branches.

Inside, Frank was sitting on the edge of the bed. He wasn't *doing* anything; he was just sitting and staring. His hair was wet. His capes and boots lay on the floor in a little puddle. On the hand that Thursday had cut he wore a black ski glove tattered by the surf, so big that it made him look like Mickey Mouse.

"What's *that* for?" I asked, laughing.

He didn't answer.

"Well, I got two fish." I held them up for him to see. But still he said nothing; he didn't even lift his head. "What's the matter?" I asked.

"Never mind," he said. "Leave me alone, will you?"

"But—

"Just leave me alone!" He flopped down and rolled his back toward me. I thought, *Okay, I'm not going to miss Frank when I get home.*

In the evening the wind began to rise. And it just kept rising. Lightning flashed through the forest, and thunder boomed, far away. The surf became the footfalls of giants, thumping on the land. Though sheltered in the forest, the cabin shook so badly we thought it might break apart. The plastic sheeting flailed and flapped. Raindrops driven sideways by the wind pelted the walls like handfuls of pebbles.

Water poured through the roof in rivulets. Frank's repairs had made no difference. In the flashes of lightning we saw the drops falling. And we saw ourselves then too, sitting in plastic and shivering from the cold. We looked up at the creaking of the trees, expecting one to come crashing through the roof and squash us.

I worried about Thursday and wished he was with me. I hated to think of him hunched in the dark, alone and afraid as he tried to keep warm.

Then I thought of the skeleton tree and how its branches would toss and bend. I pictured the coffins rising and falling, and the skeletons shaking inside them.

"This might go on for days," I said to Frank. "If we can't go fishing we might starve."

"It'll be calm by morning," said Frank. In the dark, he was invisible. "The bigger the storm, the sooner it ends."

He was right. The ending came well before dawn, with a shriek of wind like a human cry. Then everything fell silent, except for the booming of the waves. We heard the little plops of water dripping from the roof.

For once, Thursday didn't wait until daylight. He cried out with a crow-like caw as he came through the window. It was so dark that he might have been a phantom. But his talons clicked on the floor as he landed beside me.

"Chase it out," said Frank.

"No." The raven shook himself, splattering beads of cold water. "He's freezing."

"I don't care. I don't want that thing inside."

"Why?"

"It gives me the willies. Okay?"

The willies. That sounded funny coming from Frank. "Oh, the bad-omen thing," I said.

To my surprise, Frank agreed. "That's right," he said. "It thinks I'm dying."

"Why would he think *that?*" I asked.

"Just get rid of it," said Frank. "If you don't do it, I will."

I couldn't see a thing in the cabin: not the raven beside me, not Frank across the room. From Thursday's throat came little gargles and mutters. *He* could see Frank; I was sure of that. I heard his feathers rustling, and I was afraid he was going to fly up at Frank and attack again.

"Okay," I said. "I'll put him out."

I groped across the floor, trying to find Thursday. "I'm sorry," I told him. "You just can't stay."

"Now!" shouted Frank.

"Wait a minute!" The raven was twitching. I wished he would suddenly start speaking real words. *Oh, please let me stay.* But he only made his sad sounds, which to me meant exactly the same thing. When I closed my hands around him, he took my fingers gently in his talons and pried them apart. It made me sad that he didn't want to be held. But then he twisted his neck, opened his beak, and dropped something hard into my palm. It was made of metal, cold and wet.

I stood by the window, trying to find even a tiny gleam of light.

"What are you doing?" asked Frank.

I couldn't quite see the thing the raven had given me. It felt like a hollow tube, a little smaller than a lighter, with a wire ring to hold it by. Something rattled inside it when I turned my hand. I suddenly knew just what it was.

"I think he brought matches," I said.

"What?" said Frank.

I fumbled the cylinder open. Wooden matches came sliding out. They fell through my fingers and onto the floor. I knelt down to find them, groping through the old, wet ashes.

Clever bird, said Thursday.

But there was no reward for the raven. Frank leapt up to drive him away. He staggered over the stones in the fire circle, shouting that he would kill that bird. Poor Thursday battered at the window, then vanished through the plastic pane. Frank stood, panting, in the ashes. I pushed at his leg, yelling at him to move. "Your foot's on the matches," I cried. "You're breaking them, Frank."

There were nine matches trampled on the floor, all broken and useless. But minutes later we sat in blazing light. Smoke rose to the roof and streamed through the little hole, and wood crackled and split, flinging embers. We sat very close the fire, Frank holding the cylinder in that ridiculous big glove.

"Six matches," he said. "That's not very many."

"Don't blame me," I told him.

"It's your fault," said Frank. "You fumbled the radio when Jack threw it to you. Now you fumbled the matches."

He added wood to the fire, until I had to back away to escape the heat. But he stayed where he was, so close to the flames that steam rose from the fingers of his black glove.

As I lounged in the corner, Thursday appeared again in the window. His little eyes looked down at us, reflecting orange and yellow.

"He's not afraid of the fire," I said, hoping Frank would invite him down. "He must have sat right here with the cabin guy. He must have learned that matches start fires, and he just wanted to be warm. He wanted *us* to be warm."

Frank stared into the flames. The firelight made his eyes look black and hollow. "So where do you think it got them from?" he asked.

"I guess they used to be the cabin guy's," I said. "Thursday likes shiny stuff. He probably took them and stashed them in his nest."

"Or another raven did," said Frank, nodding. He had it all figured out already. "That's why the guy killed one. So he could hang it up as a warning." He put a stick onto the fire. "But there's another possibility."

"What?"

"Figure it out, Einstein."

I thought for a moment, then looked toward the door. "You think the guy's still out there?"

Frank only shrugged.

"No, that's too weird," I said. "He'd have to be a crazy old hermit to be hanging around like that."

I wasn't sure if Frank really believed the man was out there. He just stared into the fire.

That day we ate our first hot food in Alaska: seaweed boiled in water in the cabin guy's old pot, and fish that tasted smoky and warm. Thursday came so slowly down to the floor that even Frank didn't notice until the raven was right there beside me. Then he laughed. "Oh, let him stay," he said. "Who cares?" I fed Thursday scraps of fish, and he joined in the conversation with his strange little mutters and head tilts and shuffles.

I wanted to try out the cabin guy's stove, but Frank said I'd be wasting fuel. "We'll need the gas later," he said. "We can build a beacon. And when an airplane comes we can pour the gas all over it and make a huge fire."

He may have invented that idea right on the spot, just as a reason to stop me from lighting the stove. But it became his new scheme, and he talked about it as we basked by the fire, like lizards on sun-heated stones. His last great idea—to climb the mountain—had been forgotten, and that was fine with me. We drank tea made of hot water and fir needles, and I thought it was the best tea I'd ever had.

Before the sun went down I learned that having a fire meant a lot of work. We had already burned up the wood the cabin guy had left, and it would be a steady job to gather more. It would become *my* job, and I would forage a little farther every day, learning what would burn well and what would not, that old bark from the beach would smolder like charcoal, keeping us warm all night.

• • •

I got up early in the morning, eager to see what had washed ashore. Thursday came with me.

The surf was high and roaring, the waves flinging spindrift as they stormed across the sand. I saw the dashboard from a car, a Lego brick, a doorknob on a chunk of wood. The plastic head of a garden gnome rolled in the surf, its beard a tangle of barnacles.

The only thing I picked up was a tiny shoe that a baby had worn.

It was sitting upright on the sand, a little brown shoe with a white lace still threaded through the eyelets, still tied in a careful bow. Of all the things I'd seen, this was the saddest, and I couldn't leave it behind. The sole was not even scratched, because the shoe had been worn by a boy too young to walk. I pictured him smiling at those shoes as his mother tied the laces. I could see him trying to touch them, bending up his little legs and stretching out his arms. His mother laughing. But it was my own mother I saw, her hair and eyes all shiny, her smile making wrinkles around her eyes.

Thursday pecked at tiny crabs and sand fleas trapped in rolls of kelp. But he stayed nearby, and he came right to me when I called.

It was a comforting sight to see smoke wafting from the forest when I turned to go back. I could see Frank out on the point below the skeleton tree, where the waves were bursting into high, white plumes. He was standing at the edge of the rocks, wrapped up in the plastic capes. He looked like an ancient sailor longing for the sea.

I took the brown shoe to the church-like meadow, up the path and past the cabin. The spot where I'd buried the purse was already healed over, and I couldn't find it exactly. The moss had stitched itself together, hiding my secrets so well that I wondered if anyone would ever find them. I liked the idea that they would vanish. As I buried the shoe nearby, I felt as though I was starting a cemetery for children who would always be lost.

The quiet forest reminded me again of my father's funeral. I remembered how men in dark suits had lowered his coffin a little way into the ground, and then let it hang from straps as everyone wandered off. My mother put her hands on my shoulders. She was wearing long black gloves with blue buttons. "We have to go, Christopher," she said, starting to pull me back. I shook away from her, determined to stay with my father. I wanted to wait until he was properly buried, and then to wait some more because it didn't seem right for everyone to go and leave him alone. Uncle Jack tried to lead us away. "The car's waiting," he said. The men in dark suits looked at their watches. Over by the cemetery wall, two men in overalls were leaning against a yellow excavator, waiting to fill in the grave. One of them was smoking a cigarette. Uncle Jack said, "It's time to go. We have to leave." My mother sighed sadly. "Oh, Christopher, please don't do this." I looked up and saw she was crying. So I took her hand, and Uncle Jack rushed us away. He bundled us into the car, then told the driver, "Okay, let's go." At the gate we stopped to let a taxi pass, and the only sound was Uncle Jack tapping his fingers nervously. In the taxi sat a woman with a veil, with a boy beside her, and they looked terribly sad. I couldn't stop thinking about my father. For days and nights I kept seeing him lying on his back in that dark box under the ground, his hands crossed over his chest, that strange smile stuck on his face.

These memories flashed in my mind as I crouched in

the forest. It was Frank shouting my name that snapped me out of them. I hurried to meet him before he could see my little cemetery. He had brought the gaff, and we went together toward the river.

We heard the waterfall from half a mile away. It rumbled like an enormous engine, and plumes of spray drifted high above the trees. Swollen by rain, dirtied by silt, the river blasted over the lip in a curl of foam, like a wave on the ocean.

Though right beside me, Frank had to shout. "We can't get up the river!"

I nodded, and pointed to the side of the falls. "You climb the rocks. There's an old road at the top."

"A *road?*" he yelled.

I nodded again and showed him the way. The river spread right over the rocks and the roots where I'd climbed before, but we found our way up at the edge of the forest. When we reached the old road Frank's eyes became huge. He dropped to one knee and pressed his gloved hand into a pothole. He said something I couldn't hear, then stood up and grabbed my shoulder in that big glove, pulling me close. "Footprints!" he shouted.

I didn't understand. Frank looked at the trees that stood beside the road. He walked to one, reached up as far as he could and plucked from the bark a little clump of animal hair.

I didn't hear what he said as he jabbered away. But I could see for myself what he was trying to tell me.

My road was not a road at all. It was a bear trail—a bear *highway*—where generations of grizzlies had worn hollows into the ground. They had stood up to scratch their backs on the trees more than seven feet above the ground.

· · ·

The river had climbed from its banks to surge among the trees. Dead salmon tumbled past in endless numbers. They went headfirst and tailfirst, somersaulting by. But others still fought their way up the edge of the river, resting in little pools behind tree roots and stones.

We pulled out eleven fish. We threaded them into bundles and hoisted them onto our backs, and for the first time I carried more than Frank. That made me proud, but a little frightened too. Though I was getting stronger, Frank was getting weaker. At the *Reepicheep* he had to stop and rest, and he actually fell asleep on the cold stones with his injured hand shoved into his jacket.

I watched the waves roll onto the beach, their tops streaming foam as they curled and broke. There was line after line of breakers, and out in the middle I saw a man swimming. I couldn't believe it at first. He rose on a wave, then disappeared, and I stared out for a long time before I saw him again. Now a little closer, he tumbled in the foam.

It *was* a man—but a man made of wood. His arm

reached through the air, then sank into the sea again. He tilted on a wave and fell back down. He floated on his back; he floated on his stomach.

I could almost imagine that he was alive, struggling to reach the shore. I stood up to watch, and I saw his face, calm and peaceful, his head ringed by an oily sheen that looked like a halo. Then the breakers tossed him high in the air. They rolled him toward me and pulled him away. I wanted to wade out and grab him, but the surf was too high, and I was scared of the undertow, of being sucked out to sea.

The wooden man surfed feetfirst down a wave, on his back. His heels grounded in the shallows, and the wave lifted him up till he stood in the sea. For a moment he balanced there, standing in front of me with the surf at his feet, holding out his hand as though to lead me away. Then he fell slowly back and swam out to sea again. And I was left standing on the beach, looking sadly after him.

I went back and woke Frank. I sat right beside him, still watching for the wooden man. Frank yawned and rubbed his eyes. He scratched himself like a chimpanzee, yawned again and gazed around. "Hey, look who's coming," he said.

On the beach to the north, the grizzly bear was plodding toward us.

"He's crossed the line," said Frank. "He's in our territory now."

Its head swaying slowly, its great hump rippling above its shoulders, the bear came along at its same steady pace, not caring what lay in front of it. Sandpipers fled from its path.

"This changes everything." Frank stood up. That terrible smile came slowly to his face. "There's no choice now. We'll have to kill him."

"What?" I said. "You're crazy."

"No. That's the way it has to be." Frank didn't look away from the grizzly bear. "That's the law of the jungle."

I laughed like a lunatic.

"It's true," said Frank. "He invades our territory, we have to kill him. There's no choice. It's him or us."

I couldn't believe that Frank was serious. How did he imagine we would kill a grizzly bear that weighed a thousand pounds? With a gaff and a jackknife? He really was out of his mind.

Every moment that we sat there talking, the bear came closer. Each step brought it another yard along the beach. In fifteen minutes it would reach us.

"Come on," said Frank.

To my huge relief, he picked up the fish with his good hand and started on his way. He didn't even glance at the bear, but I kept looking back. It stayed exactly the same distance behind us, plodding over the stones.

"We could make some spears," said Frank. "We could sharpen sticks and forge them in the fire." He kicked a bit of wood, sending it skittering over the stones. "If I found some stuff I could make a crossbow."

The thought of killing a grizzly bear excited him. "We could dig a hole and put stakes at the bottom," he said. "A Bengal mantrap. I saw it in a movie."

Rain started falling in big, heavy drops. I listened to the tiny crabs scuttling away in front of us, as though a stream was flowing under the stones. As we came to a turn in the shoreline I looked back and saw the bear still lumbering along behind us, but not quite so close anymore. When we climbed to the cliffs and looked down, I couldn't see him at all.

The Grizzly Bear

Now Frank is on his way. I hear the sound of his boots in the meadow and look back to see a mist shimmering around his feet as he kicks through the grass.

I'm pleased to see him.

He pats the wooden saint on the shoulder, then sits in the chair beside me. North and south he looks, out across the sea. "No one coming yet?" he asks.

I shake my head.

"Still early." He stretches out his legs and crosses them at the ankles. Then he tilts back to let the sun fall on his face, and he closes his eyes.

I start reading again. But it's hard to concentrate on the story when I expect to see the men arrive at any moment.

The baby Kaetil was still alive when the ravens came. One was Cloud and the other Storm, and they were big, strong birds with beaks like pickaxes. They could have killed the baby easily, but the thought did not occur to them. Ravens are not killers. Feeling nothing but pity for Kaetil, Storm carried him away to their nest to raise as her own. Into the lining of feathers and moss she tucked him, to hide him from the vultures.

The cabin guy has scribbled right across the page *Vultures in Greenland???* I can almost see him shaking his head.

A raven's love is deep and endless. Storm tucked her wings around the baby and cried the sound of happiness. Down upon mother and child, the northern lights burned like a river of melted stars.

I love to see the northern lights. They're a shimmer as pale as smoke, a veil of blue and green. Now dim, now bright, they plunge toward Earth and rise again. Sometimes they crackle and hiss. The first time Frank and I saw them, we knew they marked a change. Summer fogs had given way to autumn storms, and now winter was beginning.

• • •

After nearly forty days in Alaska, our lives had changed. We weren't kept prisoners by the darkness anymore, trapped in our little cabin from sunset till dawn. We had turned sticks and plastic into torches; we carried fire in our hands.

Frank came in from the forest, sweeping shadows in front of him as he held his torch. "You can see the northern lights," he said. "They're burning down upon us like a river of melted stars."

Our fire had been burning steadily for three days, and it smoldered in the stone circle on the floor. A dozen fish hung drying in the curls of smoke. I had to push past Frank in the doorway because he wouldn't move aside. Then I looked up through the trees and saw the aurora shine and flicker.

"Let's go out to the point," said Frank. "We'll see it better from there."

I chose a torch from our supply in the corner. Its head was a plastic bottle, stuffed with anything that would burn. When I lit it from the fire, it burned with spurting flames and putrid smoke. But nothing could put it out. As we walked through the forest with our torches guttering, we must have looked savage and wild.

Around the skeleton tree was a growing heap of plastic junk, a little mountain held down by strips of fishing net. It was Frank's obsession to build it as high as he could, to make a signal fire that could be seen from fifty miles away. From our torches flew fiery spurts that fell to the grass in blobs of flame.

We watched the northern lights swirl and stretch, flashing blue and green. As though to add to their mystery, wolves began singing in the distance. Their howling songs seemed to match the changes of the northern lights, as though they sang to the aurora. Frank said softly, "Makes you feel kind of small, doesn't it?"

"Yes," I said.

"Insignificant."

He chose the biggest word he'd ever used to say how puny we were in that enormous world. In a way he was right. But in a way he was wrong. We had beaten the darkness, holding back with our torches the wild animals, the ghosts and the skeletons. We were the most powerful things in our little part of the planet. But in the larger world, we were also nothing.

"If I die, no one will care," said Frank.

"What about your mom?" I asked. "What about your friends?"

"They won't know," he said. "If they don't know, how can they care?" The torches made his face grim and ghastly. "Nothing will change. The sun will keep going around, and the tide will rise and fall, and down in the city it will be just another day."

He didn't sound afraid. He didn't even sound angry. I wasn't sure what he was trying to tell me.

"We're just a bunch of atoms," he said. "If I die, my

atoms get scattered around and that's the end. Maybe the northern lights are the atoms of dead people."

"But you're not going to die," I said.

"Chris, it's getting worse."

He held out the black glove, as though he could see his hand inside it. "I don't know why we try so hard to stay alive," he said. "What difference does it make?"

I wanted to tell him that it made a *huge* difference. But I couldn't think of why that was. Disappointed, Frank threw his torch out over the water. It flew in a flaming arc across the northern lights, like a comet trailing fire, and vanished in the blackness of the ocean.

Our world shrank. With only *my* torch to keep it away, the darkness crept closer. When the flame started sputtering, we fled for the cabin.

It was another cold night, another wintry morning. When I saw frost on the ground, I knew Frank had been right all along. Winter would be long and hard, and we needed more fish.

But he didn't want to go to the river that morning. "I've got things to do," he told me.

"Like what?

He only shrugged. But it wasn't hard to guess. As soon as I was out of his sight, I thought, he would start building his catapult or his Bengali mantrap. Frank had a grizzly to kill.

So I went alone to the river. Not even Thursday

was with me. He was *never* around when wolves were nearby.

I didn't feel afraid as I came near to the river. I was wary—like a deer—but I wasn't afraid. For ages I crouched beside the pool, but the only fish that floated past were either dying or dead. I remembered how the water had churned with masses of salmon, and it was hard to believe they had vanished so quickly.

I climbed the rocks at the side of the falls and walked upstream, watching for the bear. I told myself it had a huge territory and was probably nowhere near me.

Rising above the forest, the blue slopes of the mountain were speckled with fresh snow. But the river had shrunk again, and dead fish lay draped over stones, snarled among bushes and logs. I saw fish with no tails, and tails with no fish, and shapeless blobs that squirmed with maggots. The smell was strong and terrible. Massive flocks of gulls pecked away in a frenzy. I saw four or five ravens, and was pretty sure that Thursday was among them. But he didn't come to greet me. He was too busy picking brains from the skulls of dead salmon.

I walked right up the middle of the river. In the shallow places I saw the last fish still struggling, their whole backs out of the water. I gaffed them and hauled them out, clubbed them on the banks of the river, and on I went.

With the gaff in my hands, the birds scattering in

front of me, I felt hugely powerful. I was the king of the river. Eagles soared away as I came near them. Little animals scurried off into the bushes. And the masses of gulls split apart, screaming. Every creature on the river made room for my passing, and I bulled my way through them all.

Carrying eight fish on my back, I rounded a bend in the river.

And there was the grizzly bear.

It was only fifty yards away, wading toward me down the deepest part of the stream. Its head was lowered, its tongue hanging loosely. Water dripped from its snout and the fur on its belly. Its hump shifted as it swayed along.

Between the bear and me, all the birds on the river suddenly rose in a mass and flew away. They went with the sound of a breaking wave, with a rustle of feathers and wings.

The bear was heading straight toward me. If it didn't look up it would blunder right into me. But if it *did* look up it would see me blocking its path, and what would happen then?

Through my mind whirled things I had read and things I'd been told: Never run from a bear. Stand your ground. Play dead. Fight back. Then the bear lifted its head, and our eyes met.

Its muzzle thrust forward, its eyes squinted. Slowly,

it rose to its hind legs, just as it had on the first day I'd seen it. *He can't see very well,* Frank had said then. *Don't move,* he'd told me.

The bear opened its mouth and roared. I saw its teeth, its dark gums, the black tunnel of its throat.

Make yourself look small. Make yourself look big. Scream and shout. Wave your arms. Back away slowly. I had heard every imaginable bit of advice, but still had no idea what to do.

The bear fell again to its four feet, splashing into the river.

I thought of the fish that I carried on my back, that wet and slimy cluster of salmon. They reeked of blood, of rot and flesh. To the bear, I must have smelled delicious.

It stepped forward.

I stepped back.

For a moment, again, we stared at each other. As the bear swung its head, the hairs bristled on its back like a porcupine's needles. With a bellowing roar, it started running toward me.

It came faster than I would have believed was possible. It *galloped* through the water, its muscles heaving, its feet churning foam from the river. Before I could even raise my arms to protect myself, it was right in front of me.

And then, just inches away, it planted its front feet in the riverbed and slid to a stop. Gravel piled up in front of its paws, and the river flowed gray from the silt and the dirt it had kicked up.

I was still holding the gaff. I was still holding the fish. Our eyes were almost level, and all I could do was stare right back at the bear. I was too petrified to look away.

I smelled its breath, hot and fishy. I trembled as it gnashed its teeth, a sound like stones being knocked together.

I trembled until I thought I might fall to pieces. If the bear was going to kill me, there was nothing I could do. I couldn't outrun it; I couldn't fight it. I felt like screaming, but I couldn't even do that. I let my eyes close. I let my head sag and my hand fall to my side. I felt the rope unwind from my fist, and the salmon slide down my back to the river. I whispered, "Please don't kill me."

The bear roared. It snapped its teeth again with that terrible sound. The gaff flew out of my hand as I tripped on the stones. I thumped flat in the shallows, shocked for a moment by the coldness of the water. Sprawled on my back, I tried to squirm away across the gravel, over the rotted corpses of the fish. I had become one of them, a desperate thing trying to swim where there wasn't water.

Step by step, the bear came closer. It sniffed at my foot, at my leg, at my stomach. I could see its nostrils twitching; I could hear its breath going in and out. I lay as still as I could as the river flowed around me.

The bear straddled my legs with its paws. It sniffed at my chest; it sniffed at my shoulder. I thought I had never seen anything so big and so frightening. The bear was enormous, its legs like stumps. I saw the long, thick hairs on its chest, the short bristles on its muzzle, the black curl of its lips.

I closed my eyes as its nose touched my chin. Its lips brushed my neck. I breathed in the air that it breathed out. As it snuffled and sniffed, I began to cry. I sobbed.

The fur on its chin rubbed across my cheek. Its hot breath whooshed over my eyes.

"Please don't," I said again.

Maybe it understood. Maybe not. If it thought like Frank, it was merely satisfied; it had made it very clear who owned the river, whose territory we were in. It had stood its ground, and now could leave.

With one more roar, it raised its head and backed away. When I dared to open my eyes it was already plodding up the river. But I didn't move, even after it passed out of sight again, not for a long time later. I just lay in the icy water, looking up at the sky and the tree-tops, at the mountain with snow on its peak.

Then I collected my gaff, and I gathered my fish, and I trudged downstream.

Down to the falls, then down to the pool, then along the beach, I couldn't stop shivering. I felt the touch of the bear's lips and fur; I smelled its breath. I thought these things would never leave me, as though I'd been branded.

When a shadow flickered across the beach I looked up. High above my head a raven circled. A thousand feet in the air, it was just a small black shape. But I was sure it was Thursday, keeping watch over me.

Half a mile from the wreck of the *Reepicheep*, I could still feel the touch of the bear on my skin. I still felt every bit as frightened as I had then. A hundred times I'd looked back to make sure it wasn't following me. A hundred times I'd seen only the empty beach, with the waves folding up along the shore in their steady rows. And now I looked again.

And there was the bear.

Over the stones, over the logs, it came steadily along my trail. I went faster, but so did the bear. I dropped my fish, hoping that would satisfy it, and doubled my pace. All I wanted was to get away from it. I could not stand the thought of seeing it coming at me again. But the bear was less than a quarter mile behind me when he passed the fish, without stopping.

By then I could see the wreck. The cliffs behind it soared up to the forest like the walls of a castle. With no hope of climbing them, no chance of reaching the cabin, I headed for the wreck instead. For the last few yards I ran as fast as I could, slipping in my stupid castaway shoes. In a glance back I saw the bear running too, loping along the beach.

I crawled underneath the *Reepicheep* and up through the hole that had been punched in the hull, into the fishhold of that poor little boat. It was high enough that I could stand up straight, below the thick beams that held the deck. Right above me was the hatch, with a huge log lying across it. Light came through there, and through the cracks between the planks. I stood in the shadows, listening for the bear.

I heard him coming nearer.

Stones rumbled and clattered. A log rolled on the beach with a hollow sort of thump.

I put my hands on the planks and peered through one of the cracks. I saw the bear right in front of me, its nose held up, sniffing along the boat.

I reeked of fish. The sleeves of my shirt were covered with slime. The back was clotted with salmon blood, and I was drenched with the water of a river turned gray by rotted flesh.

The bear put its nose right to the boat. The only thing between us was the old planking. An inch away, the bear snuffled greedily, sucking up my smell. Then he stepped away.

I looked down at the bottom of the boat, strewn with gravel and sand and bits of shells. I looked up at the log and the rim of the hatch. I looked all around the fishhold for a long sliver of wood, and I found one near my feet, where the log had punctured the hull and shattered three planks. I pulled it loose, then waited for the bear, watching the bands of light in the planks. I saw them darken as the bear passed in front of me.

I heard it sniff and snuffle again. I heard the tiny rubbing sound of its nose on the wood.

I slipped the point of my splinter into the crack. I took a breath, then shoved it forward as hard as I could. I drove it out through the planks, into the snout of the grizzly bear.

The piece of wood shot out of my hand, wrenched through the little slit. With a shriek, the bear fell back from the boat. I peered out and saw it rolling on the beach, thrashing its head. It bellowed in pain.

When it stood up, the splinter was gone. Blood dripped from its nose, and a red stain had spread across its muzzle. It turned its head and looked straight at me. It could not possibly have seen me behind the planking, through the thin little gap where my eye was pressed to the wood. But it knew I was there. And it understood what had happened. I was sure of that.

Its feet wide apart, it lowered its head and smeared the blood from its face onto the stones. Then it looked up again, its eyes very narrow. With another roar, it ran toward me.

It smashed its head into the heavy planks. Wood cracked; the boat shook. I fell back in surprise. For a second time the bear slammed against the boat.

Then its claws came through one of the cracks. Just the tips appeared, white and sharp, twitching as they groped like a vampire's fingers. They slid along with a rasping little sound that made my back shiver. But the bear pulled away, and the stones rattled as it walked around the boat.

It found its way underneath. I heard it clawing at the gravel, trying to dig out a passage. And soon, through the hole in the floor, I saw the gravel moving, falling into a pit that the bear was digging underneath me.

Its claws squealed on the rock. The floor heaved up against my feet.

The bear was right below me, tunneling into the beach. I stomped my feet on the floor, and for a moment it stopped. But then it started again, and the gravel kept flowing away, the pit getting deeper.

The claws appeared, raking through the gravel. A shaggy paw reached closer and closer.

The boat tilted. Just a tiny little bit, it rolled toward the bear. The huge log shifted on the hatch, and flakes of shell and sand came drifting down.

The digging stopped. I squinted through the planks and saw the bear lying on the beach, sprawled across the stones like an enormously fat old man. I imagined it trying to figure out what to do, how to get inside the boat. Or was it now content to lie and wait—for however long it took—knowing that sooner or later I would have to come out?

Shadows turned and stretched as the sun went by. The tide began to rise again. And still the bear lay on the beach. Wave after wave after wave came crashing up onto the stone, each one a little higher.

Hours passed before I heard a raven calling. I looked up through the hatch as Thursday appeared, drifting sideways on the wind. His long flight feathers curled and shifted as he kept himself level. His head tilted, and sunlight glinted on his eyes. Then he drew back his wings and dropped down to the boat, landing on the edge of the hatch.

I got to my feet and reached up, stroking the soft little feathers on his belly. He spoke to me first in his raven language, and then with real words, amazingly clear.

You're finished. He puffed his wings. He tipped his head.

He was just making sounds, I assured myself. He was just repeating what he'd heard from the cabin guy. But he seemed too much like a prophet, like a little seer come to tell my future.

He crouched down and scraped my arm with his beak. It was a gentle, soothing thing to do, and I tickled the hairs on his nostrils. He always liked when I did that.

With a little cry he straightened up again. Like a rooster, he raised himself on his feet, with his wings flapping, and he started to shout—in raven again. He muttered and shouted as loudly as he could.

A moment later, the boat shook. There was a terrible crack of wood, a grinding of logs. The bear was back.

My raven kept screaming. The bear clawed at the

planks. The darkened shadow it cast on the hull spread higher and higher, blotting out the light all the way to the top of the hull.

I was sure that the raven was shouting in fright. I couldn't imagine any other reason. But I wished he would stop, because his cries were only drawing the bear toward the hatch.

From foot to foot, the raven hopped above me. His mouth wide open, he kept shouting his strange little cries. The boat groaned and shifted again. Then the raven flew away, and into its place came the bear. That huge, fur-covered head loomed above me. A paw reached down.

I dropped to the floor. The bear's claws slashed above me, back and forth. With a grunt and a snarl, the bear changed its position and reached farther into the boat.

I backed into the corner. The bear swatted at me, roared, and tried again. Then it pulled up its paw and drew away from the hatch, and for a moment everything was quiet. But the silence exploded again into fury and noise as the bear hurled itself against the log that covered the hatch.

It was a huge old tree. In the forest, it must have stood more than a hundred feet tall. Where it rested on the boat it was six feet across. But the bear moved it easily, though only an inch or two. It moved it again—another inch—throwing its whole weight against the wood.

No other sounds came from Thursday. I couldn't tell if he had flown away or if he was perched somewhere nearby, silent and waiting. It was a strange image I had—that black bird atop a white log, watching as the bear tried to kill me.

Until the sun went down, until darkness came, the bear kept bashing at the log. When it stopped, I couldn't see a thing. I couldn't tell if it had shifted the log, if it had widened the hole enough to get through, or even if it had given up and gone away. There was no sound but the wind, and the waves on the beach.

I lay on the bottom of the boat with no idea where the bear would attack next. Every time I dared to think it might have gone away, I heard the clinking of stones or the rumble of a log. I knew the bear was moving then. But where was it going? That was the worst thing of all, not knowing where it would next appear. Would he try to get in from above or up from below? I didn't dare stand underneath the hatch, and I didn't dare lie too close to the hole. I had just a tiny space to huddle in.

There was a clinking, a rattling of stones, then no sound at all. Without moving a muscle, barely breathing, I waited. I clenched my fists, as though that could somehow help me hear. I was sure the bear had gone.

I crawled back to the side of the boat and pressed my ear against the planks. The surf was so loud that it thrummed in the wood. I heard another noise too, a faint trickle of water that puzzled me at first. But then, with a chill, I realized it was the sound of tiny crabs scuttling for safety under the stones. And suddenly the bear banged against the boat, knocking me backward, shifting the entire wreck. Above me, the enormous log rumbled across the hatch. The bear clawed at the planks on the side of the boat. One of them tore loose.

With a machine-gun sound, old nails popped and broke as the plank peeled away from each rib. A hole four inches high stretched from one end of the boat to the other.

Through the gap I saw the surf, a phosphorescent glow that flared with every breaking wave. There wasn't enough light for me to see the bear. But its enormous mass loomed in front of me. I saw a tiny glint against its claws as they reached inside again. Another plank sprang loose, with a creak of wood and nails.

I fled up through the hatch, squirming past the log. The green glow of the surf flashed all along the beach.

Over the logs I ran. I stumbled from one to another and fell into the spaces between them. But up I got and ran again, bumbling along like a terrified scarecrow. I could hear the bear tearing at the wreck of the *Reepicheep*, but I didn't stop running till I reached the cliffs.

For a few moments I rested, leaning against the rock as I breathed huge breaths. Then I pulled myself up through the darkness, crawling on the ground. When the moon rose at last behind tattered clouds, I got to my feet and ran the rest of the way to the cabin.

Near the end of the trail, I heard Frank shouting. Something banged and clattered. Frank cried again, "Get out!"

I stopped at the edge of the clearing. The cabin window flashed red and yellow from the light of a fire. Inside, Frank was screaming.

The bear had got him; I was sure of that. It had come through the forest and reached the cabin before me.

Run away, I told myself. *You can't fight a bear; you can't help Frank.* It would only mean both of us dying. *I don't even like him*, I thought. *I wish he was dead.* I had a million reasons to run away and leave him. Why they suddenly all meant nothing, I didn't understand. I grabbed a hefty stick from the little pile against the wall and charged toward the door.

It was closed. I smashed right into it, shattering the latch and bending the door back on its hinges. I fell into the cabin, sprawling across the floor.

Frank was standing on the bed with a torch in his hand. Its flame gouted up toward the ceiling in a curl of black smoke. Thursday was huddled high in the corner, where I'd never seen him before, all twisted around with his talons gripping the very top of the wall. They both stared at me, astonished.

"What do you think you're doing, you moron?" said Frank.

Breathless from running, my heart still racing with fear, I lay on the cold ashes looking up at him. "Where's the bear?"

"The *bear*?" he asked.

"You were shouting," I said.

"At your raven." He swung the torch toward the bird.

"Don't do that!" I told him.

Thursday—with a shriek—cowered back in his corner. Frank poked at him again with the torch. "Stop!" I shouted. But it was too late. Poor Thursday, thrashing his wings, dropped from the wall and escaped through the window.

"That bird tried to kill me," said Frank.

Nothing made much sense to either of us. I closed the door, wedging it shut, then turned to see Frank looming right in front of me, his torch nearly scorching the ceiling.

"Look at me!" He lowered the torch and turned his head. There were little red scratches on his neck, a small drop of blood. "Look. The raven did that," he said. "I was asleep. It *pounced* on me, Chris. It—"

"I met the bear," I said. "It attacked me. Twice. The first time, it knocked me down in the river."

Even Frank realized that his scratches seemed ridiculous compared to that. He sat on the bed. "What happened?"

"It came running at me," I said. "I fell down and

it sniffed me. It sniffed me all over, then went away and—"

"Bluff charge," said Frank. "That's not unusual for a grizz. They run at you, then stop at the last minute. They try to scare you."

"It works," I said. "I went down the river and I thought it was gone, but it came after me. It followed me up the beach, all the way to the *Reepicheep.*"

As I told Frank what had happened, he let the torch tilt in his hands until it came dangerously close to the old wooden table. I took it from him and built a real fire in the circle of stones, wanting to fill the cabin with light and heat. Kneeling by the ashes, I saw matches scattered across the floor. Their heads were black and burnt.

"Blame your raven for that," said Frank, catching me looking at the matches. "I couldn't light the torch with him pecking at me. Lucky for him there's still one left."

One left. After the terror of the grizzly bear and my flight through the night, the loss of the matches was almost too much. To me, they looked like little fallen soldiers. They were the most important things in our world, the only defense against cold and hunger. I found the nearly empty cylinder under the table and closed it tightly.

"I feel so sick," said Frank. "I feel just awful." He turned toward the bed, and I saw his black glove lying on top of the mattress.

As though he'd forgotten that he wasn't wearing it, he snatched it up and put it on.

"Let me see your hand," I said.

"No."

Frank kept it hidden. In the firelight and shadows, I caught just a glimpse of purple, swollen fingers. Then he stretched out on the bed, his face toward the wall.

"Don't let the raven come in," he said. "Please, Chris. Promise you'll keep it out."

12

My Father's Ghost

A glint of light shines from the water. Again, for a moment, I'm sure people have come to save us.

But it's only the tip of a wave catching the sun, a flash that's there, then gone.

Suddenly a loneliness fills me up from inside. I'm not sure if it comes from the empty sea or only from my memories. It makes me sad to remember that night, when Thursday flew from the cabin. Driven away by Frank, abandoned by me, he must have felt betrayed.

I should have gone looking for him. But I was too scared of the bear to go out in the forest. I couldn't forget the touch of its nose, the hot smell of its breath, the sound of its teeth snapping together. I didn't leave the fire all night.

I remember how I sat there, staring into the flames as

I tried to sort out what had happened. I kept wondering why Thursday had left me at the *Reepicheep*. Just to fly to the cabin to attack Frank? That made no sense, although Frank had the cuts on his neck to prove it. But I thought there was another, better explanation. Maybe the raven had gone for help. What if he was only trying to make Frank get up from the bed, to follow him back to the *Reepicheep*, and no one would listen to him?

Poor Thursday. What I wouldn't give right now to hear the whistle of his flight, to see him gliding across the meadow toward me. I love the way his wings flare at their tips as he stops in midair. I want him to stand beside me and speak his funny little words again.

Beside me, Frank is holding out his hand impatiently. He snaps his fingers. "Come on," he says, as though he's said it a hundred times already. "Give me the book. I'll read it aloud."

I pass him *Kaetil the Raven Hunter*. His finger slips in beside mine as though he means to keep my place. But he takes only a glance at the page, then shuffles through the book to find the point where he had stopped reading.

Then he wriggles into his chair and begins.

Kaetil sat on a stone in the high meadow and sharpened the barbs his ravens wore. The final battle was coming soon. He could smell it in the air, like the scent of smoke from a fire he could not see.

Frank turns the page and keeps reading. His voice becomes a droning sound as my mind drifts back to the cabin.

• • •

That night when Frank was sick, I fell asleep thinking of grizzly bears. But I was woken by my father.

I heard his voice calling to me from very far away, and when I opened my eyes I could still hear a distant echo.

From shimmering coals in the fire circle, gray smoke twisted toward the ceiling. My father appeared inside it, like a shadow without a shape, as though I was seeing him through pebbled glass. He wore clothes as ragged as the scraps of cloth that hung from the skeleton tree.

It was not the same thing at all as the night his ghost had come to the house. To see him looming gray and gauzy in the smoke made me afraid. When he talked, his voice was like Thursday's, a sound not quite human.

"Christopher."

The red glow of the coals lit him up in patches as the smoke gusted around him.

"Watch for a man," he told me.

Frank was asleep on the bed, the dark hump of his body covered by cloth and plastic.

"A man," said my father. A groan came from his ghost—his spirit—whatever it was. "A man will arrive."

He faded away, then slowly reappeared, holding his hand toward me. "Seven days later, you'll be saved."

His body grew thin and transparent, wavering in the whorls of heat.

"Dad!" I got up from the floor, trying to take his hand in mine. But it became a plume of smoke that whirled away and disappeared.

And that was how I woke, standing by the fire with my hands held in the smoke. The window was utterly black; it wasn't even close to morning. Frank was staring at me from the bed.

"What are you doing?" he asked.

"I saw my dad," I told him. "I saw him in the smoke. He was right here."

Frank looked suddenly afraid, as though he was the one who had seen the ghost. He shook his head and told me, "You were dreaming. I saw you get up."

"But it was so real." I rubbed my arms; they were cold. "He told me to watch for a man. He said a man will arrive, and seven days later we'll be saved."

"If a man arrives, we'll be saved right then," said Frank. "Why wait seven days?"

I had no answer for that. I wondered if I really had been only dreaming.

"Smoke looks weird sometimes," said Frank. "It kind of steals your mind."

Uncle Jack had told me the same thing, and it was

clear that Frank didn't want to talk anymore about ghosts. He just sat there staring, looking pale and small.

But I knew what I'd seen. I didn't understand it, but I believed that my father had actually come to the cabin in one form or another. It was an idea that scared me as much as it gave me hope.

"I'm cold," said Frank. He asked me to build a big fire, and soon the cabin was sweltering hot. But he couldn't stop shivering. His teeth chattered in quick bursts, as loud as a woodpecker's tapping.

I spread my poncho on top of him, the space blanket too, and all the plastic sheets we had gathered from the beach. But still he shivered, his whole body shaking. I took a stone from the fire circle and tucked it against his body. Frank was hotter than the stone.

I didn't hear the raven come to the window. I looked up and there he was, his head and shoulders poking through the plastic, the rest of him still outside. He kept turning his head, watching me as I picked up another stone and put it in place. For a long time he peered at Frank, so intently that it scared me.

Somehow, Frank sensed the raven was there. He turned his head toward the window, then raised his hands in fright. They tangled in the plastic blankets, as though his arms had become wings. "No," he cried. "No!"

Frank made me pile the fire so high and hot that it

scorched the salmon hung above it. He kept his jacket on and wrapped himself up in the foam mattress. But still he shivered.

Thursday woke me in the night. I heard his shout and saw his head thrust through the plastic window. He looked down at me, across at Frank, but would not come inside. I didn't even *try* to tempt him. Drenched with sweat, I could hardly breathe from the heat. The fire roared and sparks flew everywhere. They had melted holes in the plastic roof. They had made deep craters in the foam mattress.

Frank lay sprawled across the bed, and an awful smell filled the cabin. I thought the fish had gone rotten again. It was that same sort of stink, of maggots and dead flesh. I got up to look.

Frank was asleep, and he looked awful. The firelight on his pale face gave him the same unnaturally rosy glow that I'd seen painted on the face of my dead father. He had taken off the black glove. It lay on his chest like a severed hand, still holding its shape.

Thursday watched me from the window, only his head inside the cabin. I kicked the fire apart to make it smaller, then broke off a few pieces of salmon. They were dry and hard, as red as lipstick. There was nothing wrong with the fish. I gave a chunk to Thursday, who gobbled it down on the windowsill.

Frank moaned. He rolled over, his arms flopping, and I saw his injured hand. I nearly screamed.

It was puffy, like an old mushroom. Streaks of red ran up his wrist and along his arm, and the torn flesh around the raven's wounds was black like old meat. Frank's hand was rotting.

I stood over him for a moment and watched him sleep. His eyelids twitched, and I could see the white slits of his eyeballs. As my mother would have done for me, I reached down to feel his forehead.

He came awake. Startled to see me looming above him, he flinched, and the black glove tumbled from his chest. That awful, rotten hand swung up to push me away. We looked at each other, and then Frank tried frantically to hide that hand inside his jacket.

But he knew I'd seen it, and now he brought it out again and held it up. His face, always so much like a mask, showed his fear and disgust.

"Oh, Chris, I'm scared," he said.

Well, of course he was scared. But I could hardly imagine the courage it took Frank to *say* he was scared. It was probably the first time in his life he had told anyone that. I felt that I had seen inside him.

"It hurts so bad." He sat up on the edge of the bed, that awful thing lying on his lap. "It's like being stabbed with a hot knife. But it never stops."

I sat beside him. I put my arm around his shoulder.

I thought he might push me away—I was ready for that—but he didn't. He leaned against me, not quite crying, but very close.

"I'm so cold," he said.

Thursday shrieked. His wings drummed on the plastic as I held Frank tighter. The bird made a terrible racket. "He's jealous," I said. Then Frank pulled away, and we both were a bit embarrassed. But the raven fell quiet. He looked at Frank in a curious way, with his round eyes fluttering. *Death and ravens go together.* I remembered Frank telling me that, and I wondered if it was true. A moment later, Thursday slipped out through the window and flew away.

I brought water for Frank. I took stones from the fire circle and tucked them around him. His skin felt hotter than the stones, but he still shivered and talked of the cold. Greasy with sweat, he twisted and turned. Around dawn, he fell asleep so suddenly that I thought he had died. I couldn't see him breathing. I had to press my hand on his chest to feel his heart—a fluttery thing as quick as the raven's.

His eyes were half open. I was surprised by their color, as brown as the deepest water in the fishing pool. My father's eyes had been like that, so dark they were nearly black. As I stared, Frank turned his head a little, and I felt a shock as our eyes met. It seemed that we linked together, that I could see right through his eyes and into his thoughts, and that he could do the same with me. I felt his fear, his loneliness, and pulled myself away.

Through the plastic blankets, Frank's hot fingers

squeezed my wrist. He tried to draw me down toward him, but I couldn't bear to look into his eyes again. "I'll get you water," I said, standing up.

His hand flopped back onto the mattress.

I held a bottle to his lips. But the water only spilled away. I tore a piece of foam from the corner of the mattress and soaked it like a sponge. When I dabbed it at his lips, Frank sucked like a child, his lips curling greedily over the foam.

All morning I sat with him, nearly faint from the heat as the fire raged. Remembering how my mother and father had looked after me when I was sick, I dabbed water on Frank's face and neck. I brushed his hair from his eyes.

He's going to die. I didn't want to think about that, but I couldn't stop. What would I do if that happened? I imagined Frank lying stiff and cold, just a *shell* that used to be a boy. I pictured myself dragging him down the trail to the skeleton tree in the darkness, trying to lift him somehow into the branches. And there he would lie, day after day, month after month. . . .

I was not afraid for myself. I just didn't want his life to end. That was why I started crying, why I lay down beside him. He was dying, and there was nothing I could do to save him.

What a mess I'd made of things, I thought. If I had been more of a help we might have made a raft and sailed away. We might have made a signal that an airplane could have seen. If I hadn't tamed the raven, Frank would not have been wounded and infected. And I couldn't even feed him. There was still sedge and seaweed and barnacles. But I could spend all day gathering that sort of thing, and it would barely keep us alive. I had gone for fish and come back with nothing. With *less* than nothing. The gaff and the knife now lay in the wreck of the *Reepicheep*, abandoned in my fear.

I knew I had to go back and get them, even if the bear was waiting for me. But there was something else I had to do for Frank, something even worse than that. I had to climb the mountain.

I went right then, before I could change my mind. I drowned the fire and stamped out the coals. I would have to use the last match to start a new fire, but I was terrified at the thought of Frank burning up in the cabin.

I took the roll of orange caution tape that I'd found long ago, closed the door firmly behind me, and walked north in my ragged poncho. With every step I thought about the bear, and the closer I got to the *Reepicheep* the harder it was to keep going.

When I reached the wreck I found it torn apart. It looked like one of the skeletons in its coffin, a giant wooden rib cage surrounded by scattered bones. More than half the planks had been pulled away, and they lay splintered on the beach. Inside, below a pile of broken timbers, I found the gaff and the knife. I grabbed them and hurried away.

Past the boulders, around the point, all the way to the waterfall, I kept turning my head. I knew the bear was somewhere around me, and I wondered if there was a man as well, the man my father told me to watch for. I heard the slithering of the little crabs scuttling away in front of me, and thought it was strange that I could frighten them just as much as the bear frightened me. I wished that I too could hide under a rock if the bear appeared.

At the waterfall a rainbow arched above the river. Dead salmon went tumbling past as I climbed past the grizzly highway and trekked up to the river. Even the gulls had moved on, chasing the salmon upstream. I could hear them squawking and screaming in the distance.

As I reached the first bend I saw a wolf. It was long-legged and thin, splashing across the river like a dog on skinny stilts. It climbed the bank and shook itself, spraying a silver mist. I felt no fear, although I knew it was utterly wild. It glanced back over its shoulder, then disappeared among the trees.

Straight ahead, the mountain filled half the sky. The fresh snow had melted, but there were gleaming patches high on the slopes, above the ragged divide of forest and rock.

For a while I just stood and stared at the jagged peak. Then I followed the wolf into the forest and started up the mountain.

The sound of the river soon faded. My time in Alaska had made me slim and strong, with muscles I'd never had before. I used the gaff like a pirate's hook, swinging myself over fallen logs.

Every ten or twenty yards I stopped and tied a piece of the orange tape to a branch or to a bush. I wanted to make sure I could find my way back, but I kept seeing those words reeling out between my hands: CAUTION. CAUTION.

I went nearly straight uphill, aiming for the summit whenever I saw it through the trees. When I came out of the forest, as high up the mountain as trees could grow, I tied the last of my ribbon in a big bundle to a little dwarf of a tree. Then I started up a stony slope with my shadow sliding along beside me. It was short and chubby, and I laughed when I saw it. "Oh, hi, Alan," I said. "How's it going?"

The thin air left me breathless; the height made me dizzy. Soon I was panting for breath. I looked down over the river, over the forest and the ocean. I found the little grassy patch around the skeleton tree.

My shadow Alan kept growing as we climbed together. The setting sun made him tall and thin. His skinny arms swung like sticks. But he was already fading away, turning paler all the time.

The slope grew steeper. I heard a rumbling noise and looked up to see a cloud of dust rolling down the mountain. Dark-colored rocks bounded along inside it. As they crashed into the forest below me, a mass of crows burst from the trees. The dust cloud grew smoky thin as it drifted across the mountain.

I climbed at an angle toward the ridge, and found myself at a slope of loose shale. It was just like the place where I'd struggled with Alan when I was nine years old. I could almost see Uncle Jack and my father and the straggling line of boys making their way across it.

My shadow Alan was now an eighty-foot giant sprawled on the shale. I raised my arm and so did he, his fingers zooming up across the rock to touch the very tip of the mountain.

"Let's go," I told him, and stepped out onto the shale.

Tiny stones skittered away underneath me. I started sliding, then fell forward as I reached out to catch myself. The shadows of my hands stretched to catch them.

I heard my uncle's voice. *Stand up straight. Don't lean into the mountain.*

Using the gaff for a walking stick, I pushed myself up. Shadow Alan moved along ahead of me, as though leading the way to the summit. He grew so tall that he couldn't even fit on the mountain. As we reached the little patch of snow and left the shale behind us, he began to fade away.

I ate handfuls of snow, crushing them into my

mouth. And then, with the sun just a red line between the sea and the sky, I trudged up the ridge to the top of the mountain.

I had expected to find a sharp little peak at the summit. But there was a flat spot instead, about the same size as the cabin floor, and I stood there for a while, feeling heroic. I could see for mile after mile all around. We were definitely not on an island.

I sat to watch the sky turn black, hoping for lights to appear somewhere in the wilderness. I saw the stars come out: the Milky Way, Orion's Belt. I remembered my father taking me outside to see a meteor shower and putting names to the brightest stars. "That's the Big Dipper there. And that's Cassiopeia, that upside-down W." How old was I then? Maybe three, not more than four. I remembered being carried in his arms, bouncing along. Mom was with us.

They were happy then. They held hands, leaned against each other, laughed softly in the darkness. I felt safe then. I felt loved, and I wished I could go back to that time and make it last forever.

The wind blew steadily on the top of the mountain. With just a thin, torn blanket around me, I shivered badly. I kept rubbing my arms, then stood up to stomp my feet. Below me, everything was so black that I could close my eyes and it made no difference. I had found the loneliest place in the world. I might as well have been standing on the moon. There was no one to help me. No one to save poor Frank.

A satellite went gliding by. A shooting star burned its way toward Earth. The northern lights appeared, as pale as smoke. And then the moon came up, so huge and white that it drowned out the aurora. I watched it sail along through the hours as I waited for the sun to rise again, the sad face of the man in the moon staring down at me.

I thought of my mother and father, of Alan and Uncle Jack. I thought of Frank lying alone in the cabin. Would he still be alive when I got back? I remembered him looking up at me as I left the cabin, and a little memory suddenly flashed in my mind of the very first time I'd seen him, his black hair flopping down, his mouth in a pout, his dark eyes smoldering.

I tried to bring back that memory. Again his face flashed in my mind, and I felt myself sitting on the black upholstery of a big black car. It was not in the ropey, diesel-scented warmth of *Puff*'s little cabin where I'd first seen Frank. It was in a huge car as it sat idling at a gate made of brick and iron, below enormous trees. I was sitting in the back with my mother. Uncle Jack was up in the front seat, and a man in a dark suit was driving. He'd stopped to let a yellow taxi turn in front of us. It came through the gate and went slowly past, and I saw a boy in the backseat, staring out through the window. His dark hair fell over one eye, and he blew it aside with a puff of breath.

That was Frank. It was Frank a bit younger, Frank in a suit and tie. But it was the same boy I had met many months later in Kodiak.

Our lives had crossed for an instant at the gates to the cemetery, on the day of my father's funeral. Now, alone on the mountain, I tried to figure out how that had happened. At first it seemed a big coincidence, but suddenly everything fell into place. I leaned back my head and shouted, like a wolf howling at the moon. In that moment I knew the answer to almost every question that had bothered me since my first day in Alaska. It made me happy and sad and angry, and I folded down on the ground and started sobbing. High above me, the man in the moon went floating by.

I could hardly wait to talk to Frank. I was excited, and nervous too, and I started down the mountain as soon as I saw the sun. I followed the ridge and crossed the patch of snow, going faster all the time. I leapt along the line of my own footprints and bounded down the shale. A river of stone cascaded around me, and I rode it all the way to the trees. I felt as though my life had changed.

On the long hill through the forest I startled a deer. It burst from a bush with its white tail twitching and raced ahead of me. I followed it, weaving between the trees, bashing through bushes, hurdling fallen logs. My strips of caution tape flashed beside me, here and there, and the deer and I ran together down the mountain. My imaginary world had come true. I was Robinson Crusoe, the castaway boy, hurtling through the forest on the heels of a deer.

It veered to the side and down a steep gully, crashing through crackly bushes. I stopped to catch my breath—and found I'd lost the way. Though I looked all around, I couldn't see any orange tape.

I listened for the river, or for the surf along the shore. But the forest absorbed all sound. I couldn't see the sun or the shadows it cast; I couldn't tell east from west. I walked straight downhill, hoping to reach the ocean.

Instead, I came to the trail of the grizzly bears.

I felt icy cold as I stood in one of the ancient, hollowed footprints and wondered what to do. I could keep blundering down the hill and hope for the best, or I could follow the trail to the river and *know* where I was. What if I met the bear from the river, or even another, bigger bear? But what if I didn't follow the trail and got hopelessly lost? What if I had to spend a night among all the bears, and the wolves, and whatever else there might be? What if Frank died because I was late getting back?

I took the trail.

It was the way Uncle Jack would have gone. The daredevil route. It was probably the way Frank would have gone in my place. But to walk down the grizzly highway was the most frightening thing I'd ever done. The air seemed to tingle with the nearness of bears, and I strained to hear the padding of huge paws, the huffing of breath. When I heard seagulls crying faintly, I went faster. When I heard the waterfall, I started running.

I had never been happier to see the ocean. I started calling for Thursday as I passed the *Reepicheep*, and when he didn't come to greet me, I feared something was wrong.

But my worries melted away when I reached the cabin and heard his muttering voice. He was *inside*. Feeling happy and jealous at the same time, I stopped at the door to listen. I couldn't hear Frank, but Thursday made his lovely little raven sounds. A jolt shot through my heart. What if he'd changed friends, choosing Frank instead of me?

I yanked the door wide open.

On the bed, Frank was lying on his back. Thursday's black head shot up beside him, rising over his chest. Something green and black dangled from the raven's beak. With a cry of surprise he dropped it, and his wings whistled open.

It made my heart sink to see them so close together. Frank didn't even turn toward me. "Well, I'm back!" I shouted, stepping inside.

Frank still didn't move. But Thursday shrieked at me to keep away. His wings wide open, his little eyes ablaze, he looked like a demon.

I felt sad and betrayed, so empty inside. I wanted to turn and run from the cabin. But then I saw that Thursday's beak was stained with blood.

"Frank?" I said. He still didn't move. *"Frank?"*

I went right up to the bed. Thursday flapped his wings and cried frantically with human words. *Clever bird. Clever bird!*

Frank looked more dead than asleep. His injured hand lay splayed on top of the bed, all red and torn. His wounds gaped open, tinged green around the edges and stuffed with a puss-like paste.

Every awful thing I'd heard about ravens seemed true. The graveyard bird, the eater of corpses. There stood Thursday with Frank's blood smeared on his beak, that same green paste bubbling from his nostrils.

"Get out of here!" I raised the gaff and rushed forward. "Go on, get out!"

I tried to hit him. I tried to *kill* him. But Thursday whirled around in midair and flew out through the door.

I hurled the gaff after him. It went spinning into the trees, and little twigs came raining down in a sprinkle of needles. But already Thursday was far away. I hoped he was gone forever.

Angry and sad, I went back to the cabin and closed myself inside. I jammed sticks and wood in the window to make sure that Thursday could not come in. Then I sat on the bed to care for Frank.

More than ever, I worried about him. He slept all day and he slept all night. Toward dawn, he started moaning. He tossed on the bed, kicking his legs as though trying to run. I sat right beside him. "It's all right," I said. "It's okay."

When I went out for more wood I was surprised to see Thursday standing near the door. He was back in his old place, where he had waited in the early days, hoping I'd let him in. He looked up at me and made his little welcoming cry.

"Go away," I told him. "I don't want you around anymore. I don't like you."

He blinked at me, looking so sad that I knew he understood. Then he lowered his head as though bowing, raised it again and stepped backward.

On the ground by his feet was a watch. I could tell with a glance that it was the fanciest watch I'd ever seen. Silver and gold, it had a dial nearly as big as a pancake.

Clever bird, said Thursday. He shuffled back another step and tipped his head again, inviting me to take the watch. It glistened in the morning light.

More wary than he'd ever been, the raven kept his wings partly open, ready to fly away in a moment. His round eyes shifted from side to side. When I bent down he hopped back, careful to stay out of reach.

I picked up the watch, surprised to see the second hand moving.

Clever bird, said Thursday, in a desperate little voice.

It made me sad that he was trying so hard to please me. I wanted to hold him again, to stroke his feathers. But in my mind was that image of him looming like a vulture over Frank.

If I cared at all about Frank, I had to chase away Thursday. By the way he tipped his head, I could tell he knew what I was thinking. He forced out three words in a croaky voice. *Want some fish.*

I remembered offering him a scrap of salmon with those same words—and Frank getting angry about it. That was the first thing I'd ever said to him. He rocked his head and muttered.

Terrified I would send him away, he was trying as hard as he could to make friends again. I knew what *that* was like, all right. To have a friend one moment, and not the next, was horrible.

He was no longer a wild animal. His only companions were people. He loved to be held, to have his feathers preened and tickled. All he wanted was to be loved. "Oh, Thursday," I said.

But inside him was a tiny part that could never be tamed. And that made me afraid of him. I could never be sure what he was thinking, never know what he might do. I shouted, "Get away!" I swung my foot and tried to kick him, but he was already rising from the ground in a whirl of wind and feathers. I hated myself for driving him off, but I had no choice. "Go on. Get out of here!" I shouted. Inside, I felt like crying.

He didn't quite clear the bushes. In a panic he went crashing through their tops, turning in the air as he tucked his feet into flying position. Then he merged into the shadows of the forest, and in a moment he was gone.

For the rest of the day I sat with Frank. He seemed to teeter between life and death, and I tried to hold him on the side of the living. I told him stories, every little thing I could remember about Uncle Jack.

In the evening the wind picked up. The trees whispered and groaned. Heavy drops of rain splattered on the roof. I thought automatically of Thursday. Then I remembered his mouth full of green strands. I couldn't get it out of my mind that he had been eating Frank's flesh.

Sometime in the night, Frank's fever broke. In the early morning he came awake, asking for water and food. When I brought him soup he lifted his hand from under his jacket.

I squinted and turned away, not wanting to see his wounds. But Frank said, "Hey. Chris, look at this."

The long, livid streaks on his wrist had faded. The wounds still looked raw and sore, but they were healing now, their edges knitting together. Frank touched them, unbelieving, and his fingers came away coated with the green paste. "What the hell is that?" he asked.

It looked like vomit, like mushrooms and moss. Frank wiped his fingers desperately on the mattress. He put on the glove again, hiding the wounds from himself and from me.

He took the soup, and I moved away to stoke the fire. He smacked his lips as he ate. "How long have I been sleeping?" he asked.

"At least two days," I said. "I'm not sure."

Frank didn't say a word. Maybe he didn't believe me.

"This isn't an island," I told him. "There's no one around. I stayed on the mountain all night to make sure."

He slurped the soup.

"I started thinking about things up there," I said. "I figured everything out, Frank. I know all about you now."

"What do you mean?" he asked.

"You're my cousin," I told him. "Uncle Jack's your dad."

A little smile came to his face as he chewed on a chunk of fish. He swallowed. He wiped his lips. "You moron," he said, not unkindly. "I'm your brother."

13

The Wooden Saint

Frank's voice drones on. He's still reading that stupid book, but I've barely heard a word. When I look at him I see his lips moving, his teeth flashing between them, his eyebrows going up and down with the rhythm of the story.

In the valley roamed a pack of wolves. On a wintry day Kaetil set off alone to find them. He had learned the ravens' way of hunting with the wolves and found them eager to help. In exchange for his eyes, they gave him their claws and teeth. What a raven could not kill on his own, a pack of wolves could slay in a moment. They would travel wherever he led them if there was a chance of a meal at the end.

Looking up at the mountains and seeing Storm circling

in the sky, Kaetil knew where the wolves could be found.
With his ebony hair flowing behind him, he began to
climb the mountain.

Frank turns the page, his hands fumbling with antici-
pation. "This is *so* good," he says.

I look over the sea and across the sky, searching for
the glint of light from a ship's window or an airplane
wing. It must be noon by now. The people must arrive
in the next twelve hours.

"There's another note here," says Frank. He tilts the
book to let me see the pages. A big red circle has been
drawn around the part about wolves.

All true. A symbiotic relationship.

"What's symbiotic?" asks Frank.

"I don't know," I tell him.

"It must be something special," says Frank. He bends
the pages back and begins to read again. His voice
changes as Kaetil shouts to the wolves. Now Frank is
shouting too, quoting from the book. "'You'll run with
me tonight, you white-fanged devils!'"

I smile and settle back. He really is a lot like my father. Or like *our* father, really.

• • •

When Frank told me the truth I was stunned.

At first I didn't believe him. I thought it was just

one of his stupid games meant to annoy me. "You're my *brother?*" I asked.

He nodded. "Well, your half brother, I guess."

I was barely used to the thought that Frank was my cousin. That had been great; I thought one day we might even be friends. But to learn that he was my brother made me angry.

"How do you know?" I said.

"Because it's true." He spread his hands in a shrug, as though he thought I was stupid for not understanding. "I came to Alaska to go sailing with Jack and my brother."

"But how did you know you had a brother?" I asked. "Who told you?"

"I don't remember," said Frank. "I didn't know your name or anything. But I knew Dad had another family, because that's where he went when he left."

I glared at him. "So why didn't you tell me?"

"Because I hated you!"

"Why?"

"Why do you think? Don't be so stupid." With that he got up and stormed from the cabin in bare feet.

I followed him. He tried to slam the door in my face, but I fended it off. The rain had turned to drizzle, and we were soaked in a moment, but we went down the trail to the sandy beach, Frank far ahead and me shouting after him. "I never did anything to you!"

His voice was muffled by the rain and the forest. "You stole my dad!"

I ran to catch up. Frank dragged back the branches along the trail, pulling them so far that they sprang back four feet and hit me. He screamed like a toddler having a tantrum. "He was my dad first! And you stole him. He left my mom to be with yours."

A branch whacked me in the face. I shoved it away. "What? Like when I was *born?*"

"Before that, moron."

It didn't make sense that Frank would blame me for something that happened before I was born. But in his place, I might have felt the same.

Frank leapt down the bank at the end of the trail. He stepped over the log that lay there, where I had found the first footprint. "I never had a dad when I was little because of you," he said. "I was three when he left; I can't even remember him."

I clambered over the same log. "Wait up!" I shouted.

Frank made a rude gesture as he ducked under the branches of the cedar tree. I fell on my knees, got up, kept going.

"Well, guess what?" I said. "He wasn't around much for me either. He was always going on business trips."

Frank laughed. "Those weren't business trips, moron."

I stopped there, in the tent of the half-fallen tree. I

wondered for only a moment what my dad was really doing if he wasn't away on business. Then I understood.

All those times he'd said he was going to faraway places, he had never left the city. He was only a few miles from home, living with Frank instead of me.

I crawled under the branches, shouting, "So you stole him back!"

"No!" Frank dropped onto sand as dark as water, collapsing straight on his back as though he'd been shot.

I walked right up to him, until my castaway shoes nearly touched his bare toes. "Did you know about me all along?" I asked. "Did Dad tell you he had another family? Another kid?"

Frank gazed up at me with no expression. I yelled at him, "Did you *know*?"

He still didn't answer. So I kicked sand in his face. I kicked a big, thick clod of sand that splattered all over chest, his face, his precious hair. My shoe flew off as well, cartwheeling over his head. Like a snake, he squirmed around and grabbed my legs. He dragged me down with him onto the cold beach and knelt on my chest. With that big black glove he shoved wet sand into my mouth. I felt it grinding against my teeth, coating my tongue. It tasted of salt and seaweed, and then of blood. Frank had cracked my lip.

I tried to push him off. I punched uselessly at his shoulders.

Frank kept pressing with his knees, pinning me

down until he was satisfied that he had proved who was bigger and stronger. Then he rolled aside and lay on his back. I spat sand from my mouth, and little clots of blood.

"I knew *everything*," said Frank. "Dad used to tell me stories that made me laugh. He hated you."

"He did not," I said.

But I wasn't so sure. I had even asked my mother once, "Does Dad hate me?" She had pulled me close and asked why I would think such a thing. "Because he's away all the time," I'd said.

Ten years later, he came into my bedroom one night and said, "Hey, listen, little buddy." My heart sank. Whenever he called me "little buddy," he had something bad to tell me. He said, "There are big changes coming."

He picked up my teddy bear and moved its little arms. "Things happen to people," he said. "We don't plan them, buddy. They just happen." He wasn't making sense. He sighed and said, "From now on things will be different. I promise." And the next time I saw my father, he was lying in a coffin. I had seen that awful half smile painted on his face and known in my heart it was all my fault. I never told anyone, but it was my wishing that had killed my father.

The memories made me tearful. I coughed again, retching up sand and blood.

Frank tossed a bit of kelp at my back. It slapped against me. "He didn't really hate you."

I turned my head to look at him.

"Dad never told me that. I made it up." Frank pitched my shoe to me. "I was the one he hated. You were his favorite."

"Yeah, right," I said. I didn't believe *that* for a minute.

"He talked about you all the time," said Frank. "About how smart you were and everything. Mom would get mad, 'cause she was jealous. And you want to know the last thing he said? The very last thing he said to me?"

"I don't know," I said. "Maybe not." But Frank told me anyway.

"It was Sunday morning," he said. "It was the first time Dad ever got up early on a Sunday. When I went downstairs he was eating breakfast. He had his briefcase on a chair, and he was standing in his suit, trying to finish his coffee. Like he was hoping to leave without talking to me. He said, 'Oh, hi, little buddy.'"

Didn't *that* give me a sting. So I was not my father's only "little buddy."

"I asked Dad, 'Where are you going?'" said Frank. "'Can I go with you?' 'No,' he said. 'I have to go home now.'" Frank tossed his hair. "That's what he said. *Home.* Like this wasn't his home, where he was with me."

"Okay," I said. I'd heard enough. "You don't have to tell me the rest."

But Frank wouldn't stop. "Dad picked up his brief-case. He said, 'I don't know when I'll be back. It might be a while.' Then he left. He didn't even finish his coffee. He walked out with the cup in his hand."

Another little piece of the puzzle fell into place. "That cup," I asked. "Did it say, 'Don't fence me in'?"

Frank sat up. "How do you know that?"

"I found it in the garage," I said. "Way after the funeral."

"I gave him that cup for Christmas," said Frank.

We both sat silently as we tried to sort it out. So Dad had come home to me with a little part of his other son. He had parked his car in the garage, got out, and then—for some reason—had put the cup on the seat of my bike and driven away again. He got about five miles—maybe ten minutes' driving—before a dump truck T-boned his car at an intersection.

But why had he driven off? Had he forgotten something, maybe something as stupid as a loaf of bread, and that was why he died? Or did he decide, after all, that he would rather be with Frank than with me, and in his hurry to get back he forgot the cup? Or did he come to the house just to leave it there, to connect the two parts of his life in some strange way that somehow made sense to *him*? I didn't think I would ever know.

"Jack thought Dad might have killed himself," said Frank.

I shook my head, hard. I didn't want to think about that.

"He was so sad. All the time," said Frank. "He was—"

"Don't," I said. "Please."

We sat on the beach, in the rain, right beside each other. The sea was flat and gray, and a lonely seagull pecked along the sand.

"You could have told me a long time ago," I said. "So you 'kind of hated me' at first. Okay. But why didn't you tell me later?"

Frank looked away, embarrassed. "Because then I kind of liked you."

That was not an answer I had expected. So Frank had kept his secret in case it hurt my feelings?

He said, "I'm going for a walk." Then he got up and went along the beach. He took off the glove and threw it away. I saw his hand swinging at his side, the wound still wide open, but no longer black and rotten. Just ahead of him, the seagull flew off, flapping out across the sea. I thought of a father who suddenly didn't seem so great.

My dad had led two lives, but he wasn't happy with either one.

It was strange that the father I'd envied so much, the one I had wanted so badly, had been my father all along. He had taught Frank exciting things: how to fish, what plants he could eat in the forest. But he had left me to learn on my own. So Frank had grown up to be a boy who did things, while I became a boy who read about them. It didn't seem fair.

My mother must have guessed about Dad's secret life. And good old Uncle Jack had definitely known both sides of my father. He had tried to be a friend to Frank as well as to me. Maybe he felt sorry for us both.

I heard Frank yelling at me from far along the beach. He seemed excited about something. I yelled back, "What do you want?"

His answer was faint. I had to cup my hands to my ear to hear him. "There's a man over here."

Of course I thought right away of my dream, of my dead father telling me, *Watch for a man.* I stood up. I saw them together, halfway down the beach. The man was not much taller than the boy, and stood absolutely still as Frank walked in circles around him. I ran only a few yards toward them before I understood why.

The man was the same wooden figure I'd seen tumbling in the surf days before. Now he stood upright with his feet buried in the sand, his back to the forest, holding one hand up as though pointing to the distant place where his journey had started.

"You see?" I cried.

"See what?" said Frank.

"I wasn't dreaming. It was true. 'A man will arrive.' I told you so."

Frank rapped his knuckles on the man's head. "It's wood."

"He's still a man," I said. "He's a saint."

"It's a samurai, moron."

Well, the man did look Japanese. But to me he was a saint, and he reminded me of the little bird feeder statues in people's gardens. He had bushy eyebrows and a serene expression. From head to toe he was stained with oil, as though he'd swum through a slick to reach us. Around his feet were shiny little rainbows that had dripped from his legs.

Frank braced his feet in the sand and tried to push him over.

"Don't," I said

"Why not?"

I only shrugged, thinking he wouldn't understand. The saint had come across an ocean to save us, and it wasn't right to knock him over.

Frank pushed harder. The saint tilted, but didn't fall. His carved expression, so kind and beautiful, made him seem at peace with whatever happened.

Frank shook his head, scattering raindrops from his hair. With a grunt, he threw himself at the wooden man, pulling this way and that like a wrestler. But the saint wouldn't budge. I knew then how the man would serve us, and why it would take seven days to be rescued.

"He wants to be our lookout," I said.

"He wants to go swimming," said Frank, still pushing. "Help me."

"Wait," I said. "Just listen." I tried to describe my

idea. We could spend only a tiny part of each day looking for ships from the shore. But a wooden man could
stand there forever, unmoved by wind and surf. He
could watch over the sea with that calm expression,
waiting day and night for a ship to come. "Admit it," I
said. "It's a good idea."

Frank made grudging sounds.

"From a ship or a plane, he would look like a real
person," I said.

"It would look better if he held a flag or something,"
said Frank. "At night he could hold a torch. Come on,
let's take him to the point."

So my idea became Frank's idea, and *then* it was a
good one. We both dug our feet into the sand to topple
the saint. But now he came down easily, practically falling into our arms. He weighed a ton, and the oil made
him slippery. Frank had only one good hand. We had to
drag the wooden man down the beach, his feet leaving
long gouges in the sand. We hauled him along the trail,
working together to keep him from snagging on sticks
and bushes.

I remember how we'd wrestled with Uncle Jack's
dinghy in Kodiak, and I was glad that I was now working *with* Frank instead of against him. We placed the
saint at the edge of the rocks, under a sky filling with
ugly clouds. Another storm was on its way. We piled
up rocks that the saint could rest against, and in his

hand we tied long streamers of red plastic. In the first puffs of wind they lifted from the ground like writhing serpents.

In an hour the wind was blowing hard and steady. Rain swept through the trees and over the cabin with a sound like radio static. Inside, we sat in our usual places, not talking, as though nothing had changed. Without a word, Frank got up and put on his jacket and a cape.

"Where are you going?" I asked.

"Fishing," he said.

I stood to go with him. But as soon as I took a cape from its peg, Frank tore it from my hands and tossed it to the floor. "I'm going alone," he told me.

"Why?"

"'Cause I want to," he said. "Don't ask questions all the time."

I watched him walk away. He kept his head down as he plowed through the wet salal bushes, and I found it strange to think that he was my brother. *My big brother.* The idea made me laugh. I'd looked after him while he was sick; I'd offered to help him, but he hadn't even thanked me. I could hardly wait to be saved so that I would never have to see him again.

I kicked my capes into the corner and took *Kaetil the Raven Hunter* from the shelf. I started settling into my old place on the floor, until I realized what I was doing. There was a bed and a mattress right there, but I was lying like a dog on the hard wooden floor. I'd had enough of that. I stepped boldly right up onto the bed and sat, leaning back against the wall. I sank into the foam, wriggling until I was comfortable. Then I opened the book and started reading.

It was the height of the northern summer, and Kaetil was six weeks old. Storm told him, in the raven language, "Now you learn to fly."

Through seven days and seven nights, Kaetil stood at the edge of the nest. His arms spread wide, he teetered there, sixty feet above the ground. His raven parents shouted encouragement, but it was up to Kaetil to know when he was ready. When he believed he could fly, he could fly.

As the sun went down, so did Kaetil.

Falling, falling. Flapping and falling. His arms a blur. His foot hitting a branch. His shoulder striking another. Kaetil tumbling now. Kaetil screaming.

I laughed. I was supposed to feel sorry for Kaetil. But I saw Frank in his place, poor Frank trying out one of his great schemes. The cabin guy had not been impressed. He wrote on the page *Oh, please!*

Little Kaetil lay bleeding on the forest floor, and his parents plunged from the nest to help him.

They dragged him into the bushes, into the ferns they pulled him, hiding him there from owls and vultures. All night they worked to heal his wounds.

There's magic in the forest, for those who know its secrets. Using knowledge born inside them, knowledge shared by every wild-born creature, the ravens gathered mushroom caps. Beetle hearts. The bark of pine. The dung of yearling deer. In their beaks they chewed these things, and in their stomachs ground them up, and bending over Kaetil coughed the medicine into his wounds.

The cabin guy had made no comment. He might have found it too stupid to think about. Or he might have known it was possible; he might have believed it.

I did.

I remembered how Thursday had hunched over Frank's wounds, and it was *exactly* the same in the story. My raven had cured Frank. And I'd chased him away.

I felt sick thinking about what I'd done. I pictured Thursday in the forest, bewildered and sad. I didn't wait a minute to go out and find him. I put the book on the shelf, pulled on my capes and went out in the storm. I looked everywhere, but I couldn't find Thursday. I searched until dark.

When I got back to the cabin, Frank was already there. He had three skinny salmon hanging from the ceiling, and he was roasting another on the fire. Its dripping grease made sizzling flames and dark smoke. I hung up my capes.

"Where were you?" Frank asked.

"Looking for Thursday."

"Why bother?"

I pointed to the shelf. "I was reading the book."

"So what?"

"'There's magic in the forest,'" I said, quoting from the story.

He frowned for a moment, then rolled his eyes. "Come on, Chris, it's a story."

"But it's true," I said. "You know it's true."

Frank kept working with the fish. "So there's vultures in Greenland? Ravens talk like people?"

"Well, it's not *all* true," I said. "But—"

"I think it's done," said Frank, poking at the salmon.

It sure *looked* done. It was black and blistered, like a chunk of old charcoal. I decided there was no point arguing with Frank about magic. He just could not believe in things like that. At least he hadn't gotten angry.

I ate my dinner in the corner, remembering all the times that Thursday had stood there with me, and how he'd loved his scraps of fish. I would have done anything to bring him back, or to travel through time and undo what I'd done.

On the bed, Frank flexed his fingers as he stared at his hand. He turned it back and forth, and for once I could look at his face and tell exactly what he was thinking. He said, "All right. If that raven comes back, you can let him stay."

"I was going to anyway," I told him.

He shrugged, as though it didn't matter.

"I'm going to take him home too," I said. "When we're rescued."

"What if he'd rather stay here?"

"By *himself*?"

"Why not?" Frank picked a little fish bone from his lips and flicked it away. "He's not a person, you know. He's a bird."

"Ravens like company," I said. "You always see them in huge flocks all over the place."

"Those are crows, moron," said Frank. "Anyway, he's never lived in a city. Why would he want to? He'd rather stay here, and you know it."

Well, I didn't *know* it, but I suspected Frank was right. Why would a wild bird want to live in a house in the city? But the thought of leaving Thursday behind made me so sad I couldn't stand it. I thought of him watching from a tree as I climbed into a helicopter. He wouldn't understand why I was leaving. What if he tried to follow the helicopter, flying frantically over the sea until he couldn't fly any farther?

Even worse, what if he didn't come back before we were saved? He would return to an empty cabin, bursting through the window, excited to see me. He would look all around, and then wait. And wait, and wait, and wait . . . For the rest of his life he would think he'd been abandoned.

From outside came the shivering howl of a wolf. I

looked up at Frank; he looked down at me. The wolf howled again, and the hairs on my neck tingled.

"Wolves don't kill ravens," said Frank. "They hunt with them. They run together, wolf and ebon raven."

"Is that from the story?" I asked.

Frank turned a little red. He suddenly busied himself with his dinner, his hair hanging over his face. I took a torch and went looking for Thursday.

I walked through the forest and right to the end of the sandy beach. When I turned back and saw Frank's torch flickering through the trees, I felt hopeful that *everything* would work out. We ended up at the stream in the forest. Frank was holding his torch as high as he could, moving it slowly back and forth to throw light among the ancient trees.

"I thought I saw something," he said.

"Like what?"

"A pair of eyes."

"It might have been a wolf," I said.

Frank shook his head. The wolves were closer now than they'd ever been, but their calls and their songs still came from the mountain.

"Do you think it was Thursday?" I asked.

"I don't know." The torch flared as Frank waved it again. Shadows moved, but nothing glinted back at us. I had a feeling that *something* was there. But Frank didn't go farther into the forest to get a better look. Neither did I.

We went back to the cabin before our torches could burn out. All night the wind blew, and old cones, shaken loose from the trees, pattered down on the roof. It grew colder and colder, and the rain turned to sleet. Even close to the fire, I found it hard to keep warm.

In the morning I thought we would both go looking for Thursday. But Frank announced that he was going fishing. The weather was still awful, with gusts of wind and rain sweeping through the forest.

"We don't have to go fishing," I said.

"If we want to live, we do," said Frank. "We need enough fish to last seven months."

"No, Frank." I talked patiently, hoping he wouldn't get angry. "We only need enough for six more days."

"We don't know that, Chris."

"Yes we do," I told him.

Frank sighed and pushed his hair out of his eyes. It was a tangled mat, like a frayed piece of carpet. "You can't go by a dream," he said. "And we can't wait to see what happens. In six days, there won't be any fish left to catch."

That was probably true, but I didn't care. "We've got enough," I said.

Frank looked down at me from the bed. "You're just scared of the bear."

Well, I *was* scared of the bear. But that wasn't why I wouldn't go fishing. My dad—*our* dad—had said we'd be saved. The wooden saint showing up on the beach had proved it. If I went fishing now, it would be like saying I wasn't really sure. If I didn't *believe* we'd be rescued, it might not happen.

But Frank was so stubborn. He got dressed. He gathered the gaff and the knife and a bit of rope. "If you're too scared, stay here," he said.

"I'm not too scared," I told him. "We just don't need any more fish."

He smiled his little smile to let me know he didn't believe me. Then he opened the door, and a blast of sleet swirled through the cabin. The fire swayed and flickered as Frank went out into the wind.

I thought that Thursday might be watching from a nearby tree, just waiting for Frank to leave. I waited for him to appear in the window; I listened for the sound of his wings. But hours passed with no sign of the raven. To pass the time, I tried to read. I turned the pages without even seeing the words, then hurled the book onto the bed and went out.

It was even colder than before. Trees bent alarmingly, shedding branches that wheeled away through the sky. White pellets of sleet covered the ground, and I could see Frank's blotchy footprints leading toward the trail. There were other tracks underneath his, huge paw prints so faint in the sleet that they were nearly invisible, as though they'd been made by ghostly animals. I could press my hand inside one of them and not even touch the edges.

Only the bear could have made those tracks. Some-time in the night, it had walked past the cabin, just two or three feet from where we'd been sleeping. I erased the tracks with my feet, sweeping them from the ground as though I could sweep the bear along with them. Then I followed Frank's footprints toward the river.

At the high cliffs the wind howled straight up from a white sea, stretching my capes high in the air. Along the beach, it tore the waves into a blinding blizzard. Head down, I shouldered into the wind.

Many things had washed ashore, and many others tumbled in the surf among the breakers. But I didn't stop to search for treasure. I was interested in nothing but finding Frank.

When he appeared ahead of me in that whirling fog of spray and sleet, it was almost magical. Just a shadow at first, and then a gray shape, he took form from the sea and the wind. One moment I saw nothing, and the next he was there, plodding toward me.

He was bent over like a little old man. Leaning into the storm, he used the gaff for a cane. He went stagger-ing up the beach as the wind gusted, then fought his way back down again. The fog thickened around me as a gust ripped spindrift from the sea. And when the fog cleared, the beach was empty.

Frank was gone. He had vanished, just like that. I started running—or tried to. I reeled and stumbled over the stony beach as the wind snatched at my capes.

I could hardly see a thing; I could hear nothing. But something made me stop in the right place, and peer in the right direction, and I saw Frank huddled behind a stranded stump.

White and waxy-looking, he gazed up as though he didn't recognize me.

Two salmon lay beside him. They were big and shiny, the best fish I had seen in a long time, and I knew that Frank must have searched for hours to find them. But now they were wasted. Seagulls had pecked out the bellies, the eyes, the layers of flesh from the ribs. It made me sad to think that Frank had carried them so far, but couldn't keep the birds from eating them.

As I held out my hand to help him up, I remembered our first morning in Alaska, when he would hardly let me near him. *The day I need your help, that's the day I kill myself.* But now he took my hand gladly, and I pulled him to his feet. I held him as he got his balance.

I didn't bother with the fish.

The Glass Fish

"Dad was a loser," says Frank suddenly.

This is not what I want to hear on the day we'll be saved. I clamp my hands over my ears.

"It's true. His whole life was crap."

"Don't say that, Frank." I can spend forever trying to make sense of my father's life. But right now, with the sun shining and men on their way, I don't want to talk about rotten things.

But something in the story of Kaetil has made Frank angry again. He slaps the book into his lap. "Dad wrecked everything," he says. "He was useless."

"That's not true," I tell him. "He had all sorts of trophies for football and baseball and—"

"Yeah. From *high school*," says Frank. "That's the last

time he was any good to anyone. From then on he was just a loser."

When I look at Frank now, I see Dad. His gestures, his habits, the sound of his voice are things I can sort of remember. He's a model of the father that I had when I was very young, the father he had known himself. Maybe that's why I grew to like him.

I wish I was Frank. I want to be the one who was raised to play sports. The one who went camping and canoeing. The one who sat on a couch with his dad on Saturday mornings to watch *World Wide Wrestling*. I never got to roll around on the carpet with *my* dad, practicing the Texan death grip and the pile driver. I would have been the boy of my father's dreams. But if I was Frank I would feel bitter now too, because all of that ended.

Couples break apart, and people move away. It wasn't Frank's fault, what happened; it sure wasn't mine. But his father became my father, and Dad did everything differently with me.

I'd always thought he was disappointed with me. Now I see that isn't true. Maybe I was never his favorite, but that's all right. Dad loved me just as much as he loved Frank, and he made me stronger by making me stand alone. I think he did it on purpose, knowing he couldn't always be around to help. But Frank would say he just didn't care, that Dad moved from

one thing to another without caring what he left behind, drifting through life like a broken-down boat.
Like a castaway.

I don't know if I should be angry or sad at the way
things worked out. I guess I could wonder forever how
things were *meant* to be. But in the end I turned out
stronger than Frank.

• • •

I carried the gaff and kept an arm around Frank, and
when he stumbled I held him up. The wind pushed
us along, and rain streamed from our capes. I heard a
constant *tick-tick-tick*, like stones being tapped together,
that I couldn't figure out at first. It was the chattering
of Frank's teeth.

He staggered through the cabin door and stood shivering in the middle of the room. In my hurry to leave I
had forgotten to bank the ashes. The fire had gone out
long ago. I uncovered the embers and breathed fire into
them while Frank fumbled with his capes. His fingers
were claws, so cold he couldn't bend them. He tore
frantically at the plastic, trying to rip it to shreds, but he
couldn't do it. I had to peel off his capes and work his
jacket over those hooked fingers, as though untangling
something from barbed wire. Frank didn't say a word.
He just stared at nothing, as though he teetered on the
edge of his old wide-awake sleep. Like a robot, he lay

down on the bed. His hands grabbed the mattress as I folded it around him.

Something had happened out there. But what it was, Frank couldn't say.

I read aloud from *Kaetil the Raven Hunter*. All evening and into the night I kept reading, using different voices to make the story exciting. Though Frank fell asleep I didn't stop, thinking the sound of my voice made him calm.

The storm ended overnight. So did Frank's strange mood, and the morning was sunny and pleasant, with five more days to go.

That seemed amazing. "In five days we'll be rescued," I said. "In five more days we'll be saved." Frank still looked doubtful, but I felt happy and excited, as though bathed in warm sunlight. Then I thought of Thursday. I had five more days to find him.

I went out to the skeleton tree, where he so often perched in the evening. The wooden saint still stood at the edge of the shore, glistening with his oily sheen. He had not moved, though the streamers had been torn from his hands. Thursday wasn't there.

I called and whistled as I searched to the south, along the sandy beach. Many things lay cast ashore or bobbing in the water, but the most shocking was a piece of wood painted red. I recognized it as a shattered plank from Uncle Jack's dinghy, and I waded out to get it. Every time I bent down, it skittered away, pulled in or out by the waves. I chased it along the beach until I finally caught it.

The little fitting that had held an oarlock was still screwed to the wood. I touched it, remembering everything in reverse: the tumbling landing in the surf; the awful hours of rowing; the shock of *Puff* sinking; and every moment I'd ever spent with Uncle Jack.

I buried the plank deep in the sand among the driftwood. I didn't think Uncle Jack would want it lying in my little cemetery, so far from the sea that it couldn't hear the waves. As I scraped out a hole I felt him standing behind me. It was not a frightening feeling. Not even sad. I thought that Uncle Jack was proud of me.

I left no marker. I even swept away my fingerprints. "Goodbye, Uncle Jack," I said.

I found more floats, more bottles, more chunks of foam. I found an artificial rose and a bobblehead dog. But I didn't find my raven. I collected two plastic bottles and tapped them together as I walked back toward the cabin. The sound they made was like one of Thursday's loveliest calls: of pebbles dropped into barrels.

Bawk-block. Bawk-block. I was sure the sound carried far into the forest.

I climbed the trail and on through the ancient forest. *Bawk-block. Bawk-block.* It was quiet and beautiful there, and the last thing on my mind was any sort of danger. As I reached the stream I saw something white rolling in the water near the bottom of the little pool. It tumbled over and over, a blob of white and orange, like a puffy bit of mushroom. I bent down to catch it. But all of a sudden, in that wonderful place, a feeling of doom came over me.

It was an animal instinct that made me freeze in place, as though turned to stone. A prehistoric part of me sensed that I was prey.

Something was waiting for me in the forest.

This was the same place where Frank had seen eyes in the dark. Like him, I stared among the trees, between the trunks and through the branches, watching for any movement, listening for every sound.

The feeling passed. But I still went slinking away, quiet as a cat. Then I turned and fled. I raced to the cabin, but it was empty. I ran to the meadow and out to the rocky point. And there was Frank, lounging in a plastic chair. I raced up behind him.

"There's something in the forest," I said.

He moved slowly, turning to look up at me. In that moment I wished I hadn't come to find him. I must have sounded like the frightened boy I'd been before, the one afraid of everything. But then I saw him smiling in the strangest way.

"I'll tell you one thing," he said. "It's not the bear."

His tone and words turned me cold. "What do you mean?" I said.

Frank tilted the chair on its wobbly legs. "Let's just say I took care of that old bear."

233

"What did you do?"

"Don't worry about it." He looked so smug and knowing. "He just won't be around anymore. Okay?"

"But what did you *do?*" I said.

It scared me, the way he smiled. I felt like grabbing the plastic chair and tilting it backward. I wanted to give him a fright, to make him squirm and kick to catch his balance. But I knew his plans never worked out, and I actually felt sorry for him.

"Five more days," I said.

"Sure, Chris." He nodded. "Five days more."

I went to sleep hungry that night. Frank rationed the salmon, but cooked a big pot of seaweed and sedge. The smell made me sick. I was so thin that I could see each one of my ribs, and the bones in my arms right up to the elbows, but I couldn't eat more than a few mouthfuls of that awful gruel.

The moon came up, big and yellow, and we heard the wolves again, much closer. There must have twenty or more, all calling back and forth. "What do you think they're singing about?" I asked Frank.

"They're gathering," he said.

"For what?"

The howling rose to a high warble, then fell away. Farther in the distance, other wolves took up the song.

"Frank, why do you think they're gathering?" I asked again.

"I guess we'll see," he said.

234

In the morning, with four more days to go, I wanted to search for Thursday at the river. But it scared me to think of walking through the old forest to get there. I asked Frank, "Do you want to go fishing?"

"No," he said. "There's no more fish."

"We could try anyway. We—"

"No," he said. "There's no more."

"Well, I'm going anyway." I took the gaff and the knife, and I crept along the trail. But in the moss-covered forest I found nothing but birds. A woodpecker cried its giggling laugh, and sparrows sang from branch to branch. In a moment I was past the stream, heading down toward the beach.

I found the skeletal salmon that Frank had carried so far from the river. They lay in a pile of kelp, with sand fleas swarming their bones. I wondered again if he had tried to fight off the seagulls, if he had tried to guard the fish. Or had the birds followed him, just waiting—like buzzards—for their chance?

It seemed an unsolvable mystery. But it suddenly made sense when I reached the boulders near the river.

Another big salmon lay there. Hidden from the gulls, it was nearly intact. Though the silvery scales had faded to gray, it still glistened and shone. It *sparkled*, like no fish I'd ever seen. I nudged it with my foot. It rocked on its side with a clinking, grinding sound, and I knelt down to look.

Frank had stuffed that fish with broken glass.

He must have gathered a bucketful at the wreck of the *Reepicheep*. From the boat's shattered windows he had chosen the sharpest slivers, the perfect pieces to fit the salmon's tail and fins.

"Let's just say I took care of that old bear." It made me sick to think of Frank searching for the finest fish to be his bait, then arranging it so carefully. I could picture the intent look on his face as he worked with that salmon. The scales must have stuck to his fingers in shimmering specks. He would have remembered that frightening time from his childhood, his mother calling 911 in a panic when she found his mouth full of glass. Did he smile when he finished, imagining the bear's dim delight as it discovered the gruesome fish? I thought of the glass shattering between its teeth, slicing its gums and its throat, tearing it open from the inside out.

As much as I feared the bear, as much as I hated it, I couldn't let that happen. It was too cold-blooded and cruel. I picked up the fish by its tail and knocked out the pieces of glass. I thumped it down against a rock, and the glass shot in all directions. It lay glittering around the pool as I threw that salmon out to sea.

I guessed there were others. Frank would have set enough traps to be sure the bear had found at least one of them. But I went a long way up the river without finding a single salmon, living or dead. Even the gulls had deserted the river.

As I started back, I was furious with Frank. When

I saw the mound of red plastic stacked at the skeleton tree, and Frank adding one more thing to the pile, I wanted to get away from him forever. But even then I couldn't stay angry. He looked small and helpless, dwarfed by that ridiculous pile of plastic that was, in his mind, the one great hope for our rescue. He was trying his best, but it was useless. I watched him fling something red to the top of the pile and saw it tumble down again. *My brother,* I thought. The idea struck right down inside me.

I wanted very badly to go and help him, and I looked for things to add to his pile. I searched for bits of red along the beach.

What I found almost broke my heart.

It was a child's diary, its pages stuck together. I peeled them apart and found Japanese writing that had smudged and faded, and now looked like delicate paintings of water and mountains. I thought about the child who had written words now gone forever. I imagined she had begun her diary full of hope and dreams, and maybe she had ended it the same way, not knowing she was writing for the last time.

I carried the diary with me, not thinking until I reached the stream that I would have to go into the forest to bury it. Then I stood for a long time, not sure I could even do it. But I couldn't throw the diary away. I dashed into the forest and buried it as quickly as I could. I shoved it down into the green ground and black earth as songbirds twittered around me. I started crying as I covered it over—but not for the girl, and not for myself. I cried for Thursday. I missed his little noises, his strange words. I missed his company.

In a way it was hard to get up and leave that place. I didn't want to face Frank and talk about—or *not* talk about—the things I'd seen. But I got up from the moss and brushed off the little twigs that clung to my filthy clothes.

A flash of color caught my eye, a color too bright to belong in the forest. On the other side of a fallen log, the moss had been disturbed. Strips of dark earth and different shades of green showed where it had been torn and lifted. Under the moss lay a band of scarlet, and a scrap of the same bright orange I'd seen rolling in the stream. My first thought was that Frank had come to my cemetery and uncovered the things I'd buried. I stepped up on the log to look.

I saw scattered sticks and a pile of leaves. I saw a human hand, an arm and a leg. I saw the cabin guy, half-buried in the moss. Or part of him, anyway.

The orange cloth was the shell of a sleeping bag. The band of red was the end of a sleeve, and out of it poked the dead man's fingers, curled and gray like mushrooms. He had been hurriedly buried, and just as hurriedly uncovered again.

I remembered standing for the first time in the door of the little cabin, seeing the furniture toppled, the mattress pulled from the bed, the ashes gouged with finger marks. Then an awful image formed, of the man screaming as the grizzly bear dragged him into the darkness.

It had buried him here in the spring or the summer. And the other night it had come to dig him up again.

I backed away. I stepped down from the log and stumbled over the moss. I ran from the forest, and the birds scattered around me.

I found Frank at the skeleton tree, still working on his plastic beacon. I shouted as I walked closer. "Hey, Frank, I found the cabin guy!"

I wanted to shock him, and I did. His head lifted suddenly; he turned to look at me.

"He's in the forest," I said. "The bear killed him."

I was now right behind Frank. "Are you sure?" he asked.

"Do you want to look?"

Frank didn't *want* to look. No one in his right mind would want to see a man half-chewed by a grizzly bear. But he really had no choice. I took him through the forest, past spiderwebs that billowed as we passed, and I showed him where the cabin guy was lying.

Frank took one quick look. Then he sat on the fallen log, squeezing his hands together. "That could have been wolves," he said. "It might not have been the bear."

I didn't believe him. It was too vivid in my mind: the cabin guy waking as the bear burst through the door, its jaws clamping around his ankle before he knew what was happening; the guy grabbing on to the table, the chair, the stones by the fire. He would have clutched on to anything that might have saved him from being dragged off into the night. That was why we'd found the door hanging by one hinge. It was the last thing the man had held on to.

Frank swore. "Let's get out of here."

"What about the cabin guy?" I asked.

"What about him?"

"We can't just leave him here," I said.

I thought we should build a coffin. We could use the planks of the *Reepicheep*, or even a barrel or a box washed up on the beach. But Frank wanted to get it over with right then. "We can cover him up," he said. "But I'm not going to touch him."

A twelve-year-old boy should not have to be a grave-digger. I tried not to look at the man, but I saw his face anyway—and I thought I would scream. Though Frank was older, it was no easier for him. He took huge, loud breaths as he tossed handfuls of leaves and twigs and moss on top of the body. He didn't even watch where they landed.

I used a stick to push the man's hand into the ground again. I poked the sleeping bag on top of it, trying not to think of the fingers twitching underneath. The cloth was so torn and ragged that I wondered if the bear had come for that—not to eat the man, but to fill its stomach with the fluffy lining of the sleeping bag, or maybe the moss that had grown mattress-thick above it. Frank, as a child, had been fed cotton wool to pad the glass he'd eaten. Could the bear have known to do the same thing?

I thought of that as I covered everything with sticks and leaves. Frank said it was good enough, and he went away. But I kept working until I'd made the man a part of the forest again. When I was done I washed my hands in the stream. I washed my wrists, my arms, my face, trying to scrub away the horror of what I'd seen. Terrified of ending up like the cabin guy, I ran from the forest.

I found Frank at the rocky point, where the wooden saint stood under gleaming clouds. A big flock of geese was heading south in a shifting line that must have stretched a quarter mile. By the time the last one passed above us, the leaders were little black dots in the distance. They honked like mad. And just as the last one faded away, snow began to fall.

Frank was still watching them, staring into a gray and silver sky. Beside him, I said, "I found the fish at the pool."

He didn't even flinch. "What did you do with it?"

"What do you think?" I said. "I shook out the glass. I threw it away."

He flicked back his flop of hair. "You shouldn't have done that."

"Were there others?"

Frank waited a moment, then held up three fingers.

"Where?"

He only smiled at the sky.

"How could you do that?" I asked. "How could you be so cruel?"

"Oh, come on, Chrissy!" He turned to look at me. "You were terrified of that bear. You should be happy now. It's dead."

"You don't know that," I said.

"Well, it's *dying*. And I did that. I told you: I'm your guardian angel."

Tiny, whirling flakes of snow gusted over the sea. They collected in the crevices among the rocks, in the eyes of the wooden saint. They lay speckled on Frank's shoulders and hair. I could see he would never understand why I was bothered by what he'd done. "I can't believe I'm your brother," I said, and walked away.

Frank laughed. "You're too soft. That's probably why Dad never liked you."

"Dad liked me lots," I said, still walking.

"Did you know he was a hunter?" asked Frank. He was walking along behind me now. "That's what we did every fall. We went hunting for moose. Sometimes for bears."

I didn't know whether to believe him. But it was possible. My father's "business trips" had always taken him away in the fall.

"He saved the antlers," said Frank. "He had a whole room full of antlers."

Cold and hungry, I sat by the fire in the cabin. Frank lay on the bed with the book while I watched the flames and thought of Thursday. Though I tried to imagine him huddling warm in a dry place, I could only picture him dead on the ground, with snow piling on his black feathers.

For an hour the snow kept falling. Then it suddenly stopped in a burst of sunshine. And out in the forest, a raven called.

I looked up from the fire. Frank put down the book, and for a moment our eyes met. Then I ran out, shouting for Thursday, and saw the raven landing in a fir tree. The branch bent, shedding snow in a glistening mist. The raven clucked and gurgled.

"So it's back, eh," said Frank, coming to join me. "The bad penny." He tried to sound uncaring but couldn't hide his pleasure.

"That's not Thursday," I told him.

Frank frowned. "How can you tell?"

"Because I know him."

To Frank, all ravens were the same. But this one was smaller than Thursday, its feathers more ragged, its beak curved in a different way. Disappointed, I went back in the cabin. Frank kept calling uselessly to the bird, even whistling. "Come on, boy."

I shouted through the door, "It's not a dog, you know!"

I heard the rustle of the raven's wings, then the

whistling sound of its flight. A shower of snow pattered on the cabin roof, and a moment later, Frank came inside. He stood behind me for a while as I peered wet-eyed into the forest.

"I'm sorry," he said.

I shrugged. *A little late for sorries,* my mother would have said. There was nothing he could do to bring Thursday back. But Frank wasn't thinking of the raven.

"That was all lies," he said. "Dad never took me hunting. He always talked about it, but we never went. There was no room full of antlers; I made that up. Dad was no good at hunting, like he was no good at anything else. It was Jack who taught me stuff."

I let Frank keep talking. He confessed to other lies too. Of all the things he'd told me about our father, almost nothing was true. He'd invented it all. He had invented a dad to replace the one who hadn't paid him much attention. *His* dad was not really so different from mine after all.

I dreamed of him that night—our real father. I saw him as I had on the very last day, as he walked out of the house and down to the car. Again I saw him drive away without looking back. Then I jolted awake.

A noise had disturbed me. Something was right outside the cabin.

I waited to hear the sound again: a slither, a shuffle, whatever it was. Terrifying images whirled through my mind. Had the grizzly passed the cabin on its way for another meal? Had the cabin guy hauled himself from the ground to reclaim his little house? Maybe he was peering in through the window right then. I was too afraid to look. Or was he climbing into the skeleton tree, to join the rest of the dead in their coffins?

My fears chased each other around and around until daylight. I poked my head outside and saw that the snow had vanished. The ground was bare, and I could see no footprints. Then I finally slept, while Frank went down to the beach and back, while he cooked a pot of seaweed.

I lay on the bed and watched him. "Three more days," I said.

He nodded.

"Say it," I told him. "Come on, Frank, say it."

But he wouldn't join in. He was using a short stick to stir the soup, holding his head tilted from the flames.

"You have to *believe* it," I said. "We won't be saved if you don't believe it."

I spent the day out on the point, by the wooden saint. I overturned an empty bucket and drummed as I chanted. "Three more days. Three days more. Three more days to go."

Around noon, Frank put a hand on my arm to stop me. He'd been shouting, but I hadn't heard him. "Look," he said.

I turned around. Frank was pointing east, toward the mountain. On the blue sky above it was a tiny white scratch. The contrail of an airplane.

"We're going to be saved," he said. Then he dashed off across the grass, heading for the cabin.

I shielded my eyes with the sticks I'd used for drumming, and I watched as a sparkle of light appeared at the end of the contrail. I saw it sprout a pair of tiny wings. In a moment came the sound of engines, as faint as the purring of a cat.

Frank came racing back with the little cylinder that Thursday had brought, our last match inside it. He ran to the mountain of plastic at the trunk of the skeleton tree. He glanced up at the plane.

The sound of its engines shifted in pitch and grew louder.

It was many miles away. It wasn't even heading toward us, and would pass well to the north. Frank must have known that. But he snatched up the can of fuel and twisted the cap.

"Frank, don't," I said. "They'll never see it."

He kept pulling at the lid. I tried to wrestle the bottle out of his hands, but he wrenched it away. Off came the lid. Like a genie appearing, the air around the little spout shimmered. I smelled gas.

"Please," I said. "Frank, don't."

I couldn't let him burn the skeleton tree. Flames would roar up from the plastic, black smoke would boil through the branches. The fire would spread to the moss and the bark, to the shreds of cloth, and the coffins would burn like kindling. The skeletons that had lain there for years would blacken and scorch. They would tumble into the plastic fire.

"They won't see it!" I shouted again. "In three days we'll be saved!"

He tipped the can and started pouring fuel over his piled-up garbage.

"Stop!"

I grabbed at the gas can. But Frank shoved me away, driving his elbow into my chest.

At one time, that would have knocked me flat. But I wasn't so puny anymore. I grunted as the breath went out of me, then flung myself at Frank's bent back. I got my arm around his neck, my legs around his waist. He staggered across the clearing, stumbling down toward the rocks. I kicked the red can from his hand.

It landed with a *thunk* on the ground and tumbled toward the wooden saint. The fuel gushed out with a gurgling sound.

Frank grabbed my arm and flipped me onto the ground. We wrestled and grunted and shouted. The last time we'd fought, he had gotten the better of me quickly. But now I ended up on top, straddling his chest. It was Frank who lay breathing heavily, his face bright red.

"Okay, get off," he said. "Come on, Chris, get off me now."

I stood up and looked at the plane. It was a sparkle, a speck, too small and too distant to show windows, or even a tail. But I heard a clinking sound as Frank opened the metal cylinder. I saw him take out the last match.

"Don't!" I said.

He struck it on the cylinder. A whorl of smoke appeared, and then a little flame, and he touched it to the spilled gas.

A river of fire swept in a second to the feet of the wooden saint. It licked at his legs; it climbed his oil-soaked robes. He stood in a pool of fire, with flames leaping from his hands and head, and the smoke streamed across the clearing.

"They'll see that," said Frank. "They'll see that for sure." He didn't get his huge pyre below the skeleton tree, but the burning gas made clouds of smoke, and he waved his arms at the tiny dot of an airplane. "Down here! Down here!" he screamed.

Flames flickered along the saint's outstretched arm. His fingers started burning like candles. High above us, the jet flew on toward the west. In a minute it was gone, and its contrail faded away.

Frank stopped jumping around. He looked at me sheepishly, but there was still a huge grin on his face. "They saw it," he said. "I know they did. It's true—we're going to be saved."

Maybe it was all part of the plan. The fuel, the saint,

248

the matches ... They had all come together to make my dream true. In twelve hours, the plane would cross the ocean. In twelve more, it might be back. Someone would report the fire. Someone else would be sent to investigate. Yes, it all made sense. "Three more days," I said.

"Three days more," said Frank.

We grinned at each other. "Let's save the saint," I told him.

If he had saved us, we owed him a favor. I filled my bucket-drum with water and we doused the flames. Though charred and blackened, the saint still smiled serenely.

The day ended with hope, but with a new worry as well. If the fire went out now, we could never get it going again. We brought in armloads of wood and stacked them around the cabin walls. Frank rubbed his hands. "Guess what?" he said.

"What?" I asked.

"It's your turn for the bed."

That surprised me. Maybe Frank was just being kind, thinking we had only two nights to go before we were saved. But he might have been afraid I would fight him for the bed. If I'd beaten him once I could beat him again, and there would be nothing worse for Frank than losing a fight. Everything had changed.

At first it felt wonderful to stretch out on the foam mattress. What a change to look down at Frank on the floor. I loved the softness of the foam pad, the warm air that wafted up from the fire. But then I started thinking about the cabin guy, and how I was lying in the exact place where he had been lying when the grizzly bear burst through the door. And maybe *that* was why Frank had surrendered the bed. He felt safer on the floor.

15

The Last Morning

Beside me in his plastic chair, Frank stretches. He yawns. "Fog's burning off," he says.

I see that he's right. The fogbank has dwindled to a thin mist, retreating to the south. I had hoped so hard for this to happen, but now I find I'm disappointed. Nothing was hidden within the fog; no ship is plowing toward us. I can see all the way to the horizon, across an empty sea, and our rescue suddenly seems unlikely.

Frank has lowered the book to his lap and is squinting over the ocean. "What time is it now?" he asks.

Until this morning we measured our time in days. Then we started counting hours. And now the minutes seem important. I glance at the watch, Thursday's last gift to me. "It's ten past one." Already afternoon. I feel a hollowness in my stomach as I calculate how long is left to go.

Frank has become bored with the book. He has left Kaetil stranded at sea and now he sits with his chair tilted back on two legs, his fingers meshed into a pillow behind his neck. "You know," he says, "I miss that stupid raven."

I want to tell him, *Then you shouldn't have got angry. You shouldn't have chased him away.* But, really, I was the one who did that.

"What if it's true?" says Frank. "That I could be dead if not for that bird?"

So now Frank believes that Thursday saved him? I wish he'd changed his mind a lot sooner.

"It's weird, eh?" he says. "I wonder if he's hunting with wolves. Or maybe they got him."

• • •

A lonely wolf was howling in the morning. It sang a long and haunting song. Frank listened as he lay on the floor with his arm covering his eyes. "Wouldn't it be funny if that was Thursday?" he asked. "He could be doing wolf imitations."

It was an idea that Frank got from the book. Into my mind came a picture of the raven perched in a tree, howling like a wolf.

I got up and roasted an entire salmon for breakfast.

I peeled off the skin and tossed it into the fire. Frank watched me, and I knew what he was thinking: I was squandering our food. But I *had* to do that. To save it would mean I didn't believe.

"Two more days," I said.

"Two days more," answered Frank very quietly.

"Help will come in two more days," I said.

It was like a little grace. After we'd said it, we ate. Into the fire went the bones, the fins, a scandalous amount of scraps. As soon as we finished I went searching for my raven.

I trekked along the sandy beach, bonking empty bottles together as I shouted his name. When I reached the end of the beach I took a stick and scraped THURSDAY into the sand, with letters six feet tall. Then I threw the stick away and sat to watch the waves come in.

I told myself that Thursday would appear before his name vanished. If he didn't, it would mean he was dead. I would stop searching.

In front of me, the waves burst in their creamy rows, pushing shallow fingers across the sand. They crept a little higher each time. When they touched the tips of my letters, they rushed forward along the narrow canyons I'd gouged with the stick. Bit by bit, they rubbed out Thursday's name.

When Frank came to join me, the letters were still there, but barely visible. "Hi," he said in a cheery voice. "Hi, Chris."

I didn't want to talk; I didn't want to look away from the letters in the sand. Frank sat beside me, and together we watched the ocean rub away the raven's name. The waves rolled over the beach, erasing every sign of Thursday. I stood up, feeling sad and beaten. When I looked at Frank, I saw my father.

He had hacked off his tangled flop of hair. His forehead was high and white, and he was smiling, an exact copy of the picture back home, of my father peering up from a lean-to.

"What are you looking at?" he asked. Embarrassed, he started tugging at his hair.

Side by side, we walked along the beach and up the trail. As we reached the forest, the rain began, and with every hour the day got colder. Soon I could see my breath, and I knew that Frank had been right; there was not a chance we could live through the winter. We were going to be rescued just in time.

Already the nights were longer than the days. When the sun vanished over the sea, there were more than twelve hours of darkness ahead. We spent them talking, and Frank told me at last about Uncle Jack.

I learned that our uncle had drifted in and out of both of our lives. In Kodiak he had made two phone calls, one right after the other.

"I was really surprised when he asked me to go sailing," said Frank, putting wood on the fire. "At first

I didn't want to. But he kept saying, 'Oh, come on, Frankly.'"

I laughed. *"Frankly?"*

"That's what he called me sometimes," said Frank. "He asked me, 'Don't you want to meet your brother?' I said, 'Not really, Jack.'"

Jack. That sounded sadly familiar. In Cubs, all the boys had called him Jack. He had wanted me do the same thing, to be his friend, as though he was the world's oldest twelve-year-old. But it never felt right to me.

I wondered would have happened if Uncle Jack's plan had worked out, if I'd arrived in the middle of the afternoon instead of the dead of night. "Chrissy, meet Frankly, your brother. . . ." Would we have been friends right away? I watched Frank poke at the fire, but I couldn't figure out what he was thinking. "Are you sorry he asked you to go sailing?" I said.

Frank leaned back as a cloud of sparks swirled from the fire. "You know something?" he said. "I'm not." He squinted through the fire's heat. "It's funny. I'm kind of glad."

I felt the same way—that I was better because I'd gone sailing, and for all that happened. I'd lost an uncle but found a brother, and I thought Uncle Jack would be happy with that. Frank curled up in the corner and we slept a little, off and on. At the first sign of light we trooped outside to wait for the sun to appear. I took the tin pan and a stick, and I made all the noise I could.

"One more day! One day more!" we shouted together. "Help will come in one day more!"

For all ten hours of sunlight, the wind blew hard. The waves piled up and hammered at the shore, and snow fell in flurries of stinging crystals. We danced to stay warm, around and around the watchful saint, shouting that help was on the way. We grabbed on to his scorched wooden arm as we wheeled around him. Our fingers turned black with charcoal, which was soon smudged on our faces. Like painted savages we kept dancing, around and around and around again.

Frank was grinning like a fool. He believed in every way that we were spending our last moments below the skeleton tree.

We drummed on buckets. We danced through the grass and over the stones, and our shadows grew steadily longer. The sky turned a lovely deep red as we whirled through the grass. Then the moon rose silvery white, and out in the forest the wolves took up our song.

That last night seemed endless. Knowing we'd be saved before the *next* night came, we couldn't possibly sleep. So we built up the fire at the end of the point, and I read to Frank from *Kaetil the Raven Hunter.* He sat in his favorite plastic chair, his hands clasped behind his head. We reached the last chapter. We reached the last page.

Kaetil stood face to face with the man with yellow eyes. In his hand was a battle sword made by a wizard. On his shoulders perched the leather-hooded ravens, wearing silver talons sharp as razors. With a shout, the man with yellow eyes came charging toward him.

Kaetil raised his arm and sent the ravens soaring. They flew on ebony wings. Up, up, up to the sky on their ebony raven wings. The Skraeling swung his battle-ax. Kaetil swung his sword. One was fast as lightning. But the other was even faster. And in the blink of an eye—

"Wait!" shouted Frank. He reached across the fire. "Give me the book."

"Why?"

"Just give me the book." His fingers waggled. "Come on. Please."

I thought he wanted to be the one to read the last little part. So I passed him the book.

He ripped out the last page and he burned it.

"What are you doing?" I said. The page twisted and writhed. The words bubbled up as the ink began to boil. Then the paper burst into flames and was gone in an instant.

"What did you do that for?" I asked.

"I don't want to know how it ends," said Frank.

"Why not?" I asked.

"I *never* want to know," he said. "I don't read endings. It's more real that way."

"You're crazy," I said. But I laughed.

The light from the fire washed red and yellow across Frank's face. He was smiling. "It's better to wonder," he said. "You can decide for yourself how it ends."

I saw what he meant. Kaetil would have won his fight and killed the man who'd killed his father. But now it was possible that he lost, and the story would never really end. But it seemed strange for Frank to think that way. I couldn't imagine that he'd read more than a dozen books in his whole life. How many could he have put away unfinished? As he took his stick and poked at the ashes of the page, I wondered if it was something he'd learned from our father. Maybe Dad, impatient as always, could never be bothered with reading a whole story. I imagined him closing *Where the Wild Things Are* halfway done, leaving poor Max surrounded by monsters. *"You can decide for yourself how it ends,"* Dad would say, and he'd turn out the lights, leaving little Frank staring scared in his bed.

I hated things that didn't end. I always wanted to know what happened to everything.

I stood up. "I've got to look for Thursday," I said.

From the fire I pulled a burning stick to use as a torch. But I hardly needed it. The rain had ended and the moon was big and bright. It would be a beautiful morning on the day the men would come. I walked under the skeleton tree and down that dark tunnel through the bushes of salal. But I didn't go very far past the cabin. In the mud where the trail forked to the north and the south, I found a footprint of the grizzly bear.

16

Thursday's Gift

"What time is it now?" says Frank.

He has asked the same thing every ten minutes. But when I look at the watch, I'm surprised. "Twenty past six." Sunset is less than an hour away.

The wind has made me very cold, and there's not much warmth from the sun. But we can't go back to the cabin now; that would be giving up. So I put my poncho around my shoulders, and we make a fire at the feet of the wooden saint. We pull our chairs as close as we can to the flames.

Frank keeps looking north, then south, then up at the sky. He reaches up to push aside the hair that he's forgotten he cut off. His face is a picture of disappointment. I'm afraid he's given up.

I want to yell at him to do something, to make noise,

to dance around the saint and shout that we'll soon be saved. But he might tell me it's useless. He might get *me* doubting too.

In my hands, the book crackles as I squeeze it without thinking. More flakes of paper drift away, falling like tiny leaves. Autumn has arrived for the book, as well as for me and Frank. Everything is coming to a close.

It is strange how stories work. I turn a page of *Kaetil the Raven Hunter* and find no others behind it. The last one is gone, torn away and burned by Frank. He's smarter than I thought; it *is* more real this way. Now the story just stops—suddenly—in a way that makes no sense. And that's the exactly the way our father's life ended.

I close the book and hold it in front of me, the way old men and women hold Bibles in church. Beside me, Frank is leaning back in his chair, not even looking out at the sea anymore. His eyes are closed. But there is still time for a boat to appear.

"Hey, Frank," I say.

He answers with a little grunt.

"This is the day we'll be saved!"

He tips his head to look at me, just as Thursday used to do. But he doesn't take up the chant. He only smiles a little smile, then turns again toward the sun.

"Hey, Frank?"

This time he doesn't even respond.

"Where were you when you learned that Dad had died?" I ask.

He takes a breath and sighs it out. "At home."

It seems that's all he's going to say. I ask him, "Did the police come and tell you?" That's how *I* found out. The doorbell rang in the evening, and two Mounties were standing on the porch—a man and a woman—both holding their hats in their hands, as though they had come begging for money.

But Frank shakes his head. "I didn't even know for three days. Then I heard his name on the TV news. 'No charges laid,' or something. I had to wake up my mom to tell her. She was so drunk she didn't understand."

He kicks at a stick that's poking out from the fire. Embers explode, showering sparks. "Then Jack shows up—just one day before the funeral—and he's all, 'Don't worry, I'll make sure you get there.' So he sends a taxi. But we get there late and everyone's gone, except the guys who fill the graves. 'Oh, I guess I mixed up the times,' he says. Yeah, right. He just didn't want people meeting each other, a big scene at the cemetery. Good old Jack."

I don't say anything about our cars passing. I should have guessed Uncle Jack was behind it all, arranging people's lives in a way that was meant to be helpful. As always, he tried his best to please everybody, but only made a mess of things.

Across the sky in front of us, a redness glows and deepens. Frank sighs. "You still think we're going to be saved?"

"I *know* it," I tell him.

"But—"

"Today's the day!" I shout it at Frank, not wanting to hear his doubts. "This is the day we'll be saved."

We sit quietly, staring at the sky and the sea, as though watching an enormous television. The sun touches the horizon and begins to spread across the water. There are only a few minutes left for a helicopter to arrive. They don't fly after dark. When the colors of the sunset fade to purple and black, and there is still no throbbing of rotors in the sky, I decide it must be a ship that is coming to save us. There are still three hours to go until midnight, still lots of time for a ship to appear.

I put more wood on the fire.

At ten o'clock I know that Frank has stopped believing. I can see it in his posture; I can feel it in the air. I get up and dance around the wooden saint.

I start chanting, louder and louder. "This is the day. Today is the day. This is the day we'll be saved."

"Come on!" I tell Frank. I try to pull him from the chair, but he won't move. I whirl away from him and reel across the rocks, twirling past the fire. The flames bend toward me, reaching out as though to stroke my legs.

"This is the day. Today is the day. This is the day we'll be saved."

The minutes go by. The hands of my watch swing toward eleven. In a little more than an hour the day will be finished. It's our last chance.

"Frank, please," I tell him.

With fifty-five minutes to go, he gets up. He joins in the chant; he circles the saint, keeping pace to stay on the opposite side of my circle.

Like a pair of moons going around a planet, we sing and dance, my brother and I.

"This is the day we'll be saved."

Wave after wave bursts on the rocks below us. The hands on my watch keep moving. The second hand ticks from number to number, and the minute hand crawls toward twelve.

To everything around us, midnight means nothing. The waves will keep rolling toward shore; the stars will keep shining. There will be nothing to mark the hour except one more tick of the watch. For all I know, it's five minutes fast or five minutes slow.

But according to the watch it's midnight . . . *now!*

I look out over the sea, certain I'll see a ship appear, or a searchlight turning, or an airplane's dazzling beam suddenly switching on.

But nobody comes to save us. Today is not, after all, the day we'll be rescued. Our dreams were only dreams.

We let another hour pass, sitting together beside the

fire. Nearly a full day has gone by since I woke Frank by shaking his shoulder and shouting his name. In some ways, it's been the worst day of all, and I see now that we're in terrible trouble. Winter has nearly arrived. Frank wanted enough fish to last until spring, but we don't even have one for *breakfast*. We have no matches. If our banked fire dies one night, so will we.

I feel like crying as I get up to go back to the cabin. Frank seems angry, but that's his way. He slams his shoulder against the saint as he passes by. It topples slowly, then crashes onto the rocks and goes tumbling down into the sea. Then Frank turns back and kicks the fire into huge flurries of sparks, scattering the last pieces of wood. Some fly like meteors through the darkness and plunge hissing into the black water. For a moment I think that *this* will be our saving, that a passing ship will see the sudden flash of fire. I watch for the sizzling trail of a signal flare. But the sparks just fade away, and everything is black and empty.

We don't have a torch to light our way. But as we pass under the skeleton tree our eyes adjust to the dark, and we see the northern lights. They're blue and shimmery, spreading like a thin veil over nearly half the sky. They soar above us as we make our way to the cabin. At the door, I ask Frank, "You want the bed?"

"No, go ahead." He sort of laughs. "I doubt I'll sleep much anyway."

He banks up the fire in the circle of stones to keep

it safe through the night. Then I settle down on the foam mattress with my poncho for a blanket. We hear the eerie sound of wolves in the forest. They're closer than ever.

Frightened and sad and lonely, I fall asleep thinking of my father.

But it's Uncle Jack I dream about. I see him again at *Puff*'s big steering wheel, and he *still* can't hear me. For once I wake early, to a terrible crash as the boat plows into that thing in the water. Frank screams.

Something clamps around my ankle and drags me from the bed. I grab on to the table, but it falls over with a clatter, as everything on its top tumbles to the floor.

"The bear!" shrieks Frank.

Its teeth are digging into my ankle. It grunts in the darkness as it drags me across the cabin. I pull the table with me, through the circle of stones, through the pile of ashes. Embers come alive, glowing red in the darkness. Then flames appear, leaping pale and yellow like little spirits.

Their light glows on the face of the grizzly bear, gleaming in its eyes. Its great hump quivers as it pulls me through the door.

I grab the chair; I grab the bed. But I can't hold on; I can't save myself. "Help!" I shout.

There's Frank. I see him now. He's pressed into the

corner, drawn up so tightly that he looks like a child. I cry to him, "Help me, Frank!" But he seems paralyzed.

Then I'm out of the cabin, sliding down the dark tunnel of salal. The bear is hauling me into the forest.

It moves faster. The bright flickering of the northern lights falls through the trees, as though blue fire burns in the forest. Wolves begin howling, and their voices rise to a barking clamor.

The bear drags me around the turn in the trail. I snatch at branches, at bushes, and they all tear away in my hands. I roll over, and back again, every move sending pain shooting up my leg. I'm afraid the bear will snap my foot off.

A black shadow flashes across the shifting shapes. Others appear behind it.

The wolves are running. They're bounding along the beach, splashing through the surf. Amid their frantic howling is another sound, the raucous cries of a raven.

The bear pulls me down the canyon of salal, into the ancient forest. There is no glint of starlight, no gleam of blue aurora below the towering trees. There in the darkness, the bear lets go of my ankle. I try to squirm away, but it plants its massive paws on my chest, pinning me to the ground. I feel myself sinking into the moss as its nose comes snuffling up along my legs.

There's a smell of fur, of awful breath, of fetid wounds and blood.

In the darkness I can't see Thursday swooping down. But I hear the whistle of his wings, the piercing cackle of his voice. He flashes past the grizzly's head and weaves away among the trees. The bear raises its head and bellows, and suddenly the wolves come crashing out of the salal. With snarls and grunts, they leap at the bear.

I squirm away on my back, slithering helter-skelter over the moss. I roll onto my knees and scurry away like an animal, dragging myself through the forest as the animals roar and scream behind me. They snarl, they growl. They gnash their teeth.

Thursday dives again and again, screaming as he plunges through the darkness. His cries drive the wolves to a frenzy.

Among the trees around me, a flame appears. And here is Frank, running down the trail with two bright torches. He is shouting my name.

"Chris!"

I call back to him, and a moment later he's bending over me. The light of the torches flares through the salal, and I see the bear in the darkness, turning to run. I see a wolf clinging to its back, another biting its heels. And I see my raven, poor Thursday, lying on the ground.

I crawl toward him and pick him up. His neck seems to have no bones, and his head flops over, onto my fingers. His eyes are open, but they're gray and glassy. His heart makes such a tiny flutter that I can hardly feel it.

"Oh, Thursday," I say.

Frank plants a torch into the earth and makes me lie down. He eases me back onto the green moss and moves the other torch above me, looking for wounds and bites.

I want to hold on to Thursday. He has given his life for me, and I wish I knew the magic of the forest so that I could give it back to him. His eyes slowly close, and the warmth begins to leave his body.

Frank runs his fingers down my ankle. "It's not too bad," he says. But there's a throbbing pain in my foot, and I can't tell from his voice what Frank really thinks. He helps me up, then leans forward so I can use his shoulder as a crutch. He pulls the torch up from the moss and leads me away with the light.

I hold Thursday even tighter. His wings feel brittle and dry, like old, dead plants. I start trembling.

"I'll build up the fire," says Frank. "You'll be warm in a minute." But I don't want to go back to the cabin. Frank helps me all the way to the skeleton tree, and beyond it to the rocky point. There we wait for dawn. I cradle Thursday in my hands.

It's early morning when I carry him to the skeleton tree. Frank has offered to help, but I want to do this by myself, even though the bear's teeth have left four punctures in my ankle, and my foot feels as though it's on fire.

With Thursday in the crook of my arm, I climb the heap of plastic that Frank gathered for a beacon. I work my way into the branches of the tree, climbing among the skeletons. I'm not sure the branches will hold me. I'm afraid of them breaking, afraid of falling to the ground, with the bones rattling down on top of me. I can't put weight on my foot without crying out in pain.

The raven feels empty, a hollow bundle of feathers. Along with the light in his eyes, he has lost whatever it was that made him a creature, a little character that could feel love and jealousy. I want to reward him the only way I can, by placing his body in the highest box, in the little coffin, where he can lie nearest to the sky, in the sun and the wind that he loved so much.

I step up from branch to branch, wincing when my wounded ankle takes all of my weight. I climb past the coffins, and for the first time I look down and see the skeletons stretched out inside them. The bones are all separated, but still in order. One more step, and I'm near the top. I peer into the little coffin and see the skull of a child looking back at me. Behind it, in the shadowed corner of the wooden box, things have been tucked away.

I think at first that they must be offerings to the

child, maybe favorite toys or pretty shells. But I can't make sense of their shapes. With Thursday in my arm, I have only one hand free to reach inside.

I stare into the coffin, surprised by the things I discover.

Here's the little whistle that Thursday had found so appealing. Here's the flare Frank and I could never find. Here's a coin and a key that must have belonged to the cabin guy. And here's the body of the other raven, the marks of the wire still pressed into its body. So this is where Thursday nested. Maybe the two of them together. Warm and dry under the little roof of the coffin lid, they had watched over the bones.

I imagine Thursday had stashed the watch here as well. He hadn't plucked it from the dead man's hand to give to me. He'd chosen it just for me from all the little things he'd stolen from the cabin guy. I can see that man now, shouting with rage as his belongings disappeared one by one.

I feel foolish and sad. So much for the mysterious shifting bones and the scratchings from the coffins. All along, it had been Thursday. This is where he'd come every night, to be the caretaker of the dead, the watchman of the skeletons.

As I slide his body into this place where it belongs, I see one more thing in the box. I have to stretch to reach it.

When I see what I've found, my hand begins to

shake. Still sealed in a ziplock bag is a battery for the radio.

Will it work? That seems almost too much to hope for. But I remember Frank with the child's purse, his hope for a cell phone. *"Those batteries can last forever if they're charged."* Is this my last gift from Thursday?

I place him gently in the coffin. I return all his things, keeping only the battery and the flare, and arrange the skull as I'd found it. I climb down the tree.

In the deep shadows of the other coffins I see twigs and moss and bits of bark, all stowed away by Thursday. But I don't reach in among the bones. I'm guarding the battery in my fist as though it's made of crystal.

Frank is in the cabin. He's crouching on the floor, rearranging the stones in the fire circle. I reach over his shoulder and dangle the battery in front of his face.

He leans back to see it more clearly. Then his hands shoot out to snatch it from me. "Where did you get this?" he asks. But already he's getting to his feet. He grabs the radio from the shelf and fits the battery into place. His hands shake, and the pieces rattle, but he gets it all closed up. Then he turns it over in his hand, reaches for the dial and . . .

And suddenly he's just staring at me with a stunned expression.

The knob is gone.

Of course it is; we'd forgotten that. It flew off when

Frank hurled the radio down in his first fit of temper. I'm afraid he's going to do it again, he looks so frustrated.

"Give it to me," I say. My fingers are smaller than his. I'm sure I can turn the little stub that remains. Then I remember Thursday playing with bits of glass, bringing me the dial from under the bed. Where did I put it? I scan the cabin. The window!

The dial is still stuck in the boards where I jammed it in place a month ago. I pull it away and jam it onto the stub. I switch the radio on.

There's a click. There's a hum. Lights flash, glowing red and orange.

I press the transmit button.

"Mayday," I say. "Mayday. Mayday."

Nothing happens.

"Mayday, Mayday, Mayday!" I shout.

No sound from the radio. *It's ruined,* I think. Frank broke more than just the knob when he threw the thing. I glare at him.

"Let go of the button," he says.

You can't talk and listen at the same time. I remember Uncle Jack telling me that. You can either transmit or receive, but you can't do both.

I take my thumb from the button. Right away, a woman's voice leaps from the speaker. "Coast Guard radio, Anchorage. Over."

I grin at Franklin; he grins at me, and it's just like our first day in the cabin. I press the button and babble into the radio, "We were on a sailboat and it sank, and now we're in a cabin but I don't know where we are. We need help. My name's Chris. I'm here with my brother."

Author's Note

For many years I lived in Prince Rupert, a small city on the northern coast of British Columbia. From the hilltop house where I looked after a radio-transmitter station, I could see the mountains of Alaska in the distance, capped white all year with snow.

I spent my summers sailing, with my wife, Kristin, and a little dog called Skipper. At three knots, or less than five miles an hour, we traveled through southern Alaska and northern BC.

The coast was surprisingly wild. Within miles of the city, cell phone service disappeared. The VHF radio became useless in the high-sided fjords. We went days without seeing another person. But animals were everywhere, and they had no fear of us. We watched wolves lope across meadows and roll on sandy beaches. We laughed at ravens playing with the wind at the tops of tall trees, and traded sounds back and forth as they mimicked the ringing clang of our metal cups. We saw killer whales hunting, and dolphins leaping, and sea otters floating hand in hand.

That world of mine became the world of Chris and Frank. Like them, we drank from ice-cold streams, ate fish pulled straight from the sea and gathered grass and berries. It seemed idyllic in the daytime. But at night, when the sky filled with stars and the land disappeared, it could feel heartbreakingly lonesome.

One day, all alone, I anchored off an island where a Wildman was said to live, a savage, hairy giant. I rowed a line to shore and tied it to a tree to keep the boat from swinging. Then I barbecued a salmon and sat to watch the sun go down. Until then, I hadn't given a thought to the Wildman. But as shadows darkened around me, as the trees loomed closer in the darkness, I remembered the gruesome stories of people torn apart. When I heard things moving in the forest, I fled to the boat. From there I couldn't see the land at all. The shoreline stretched away into blackness. But every time the boat lurched in the currents, every time it tugged at the line, I imagined the Wildman clutching that rope and pulling the boat hand over hand toward shore.

It doesn't matter if the things that come in the night are mostly in our minds. The ones we create on our own are maybe the most frightening of all.

I was afraid of the bears.

Skipper had a special sound she made when she sighted one. She was just a tiny lapdog, but the awful growl that came from deep inside her gave me goose-flesh. I would turn to look where she was looking, and

I would see a bear plodding along the beach or stepping out from the forest edge.

There was no real danger. We never had trouble with bears in all the years we spent in that part of the coast now known as the Great Bear Rainforest. The one time we ever met a grizzly, little Skipper chased it off.

As Chris says in this story, the world is not really all that empty. Here and there we came across camp-sites and shelters, even little cabins like the one the boys discover. Most seemed sad and forgotten, but one had an eerie wildness about it, and I couldn't shake the feeling that something terrible had happened there. I could never find that place again. I remember only that it's somewhere in Alaska, and it was very much in my mind as I wrote this story. That part is true.

So is the skeleton tree.

Everywhere we went along the coast, we kept find-ing signs of ancient people. Huge hollows in the forest showed where their houses had been. Strange patterns of stones on the shore marked their old fish traps and clam gardens. Enormous cedar trees, maybe two thou-sand years old, were still scarred from the harvesting of planks and bark. It was as though the people had gone but the land remembered them.

We saw the burial tree on one of our early voyages. It was a gnarled old thing with tangled branches, grow-ing on a little island in a big harbor. It held three or four coffins of different sizes, their cedar boards split and silvered by the sun, their corners blackened by rot and lichen. The highest one was very small.

According to the American author Charles Hallock, tree burials were once common in Alaska. He wrote about them, rather flippantly, in a book called *Our New Alaska, Or, The Seward Purchase Vindicated:* "Tree-burial is more in vogue in the interior than on the coast, a dry goods box, shoe box, or even a cask obtained from some trader, being a good enough coffin for the defunct remains."

The website North American Nations (nanations .com) says burial trees, or scaffolds for the dead, were used throughout America. On the coast, important people were sometimes laid to rest in whole canoes mounted high among the branches.

There cannot be many of those burial trees left standing. On the West Coast, trees live a long time, but none lives forever. I feel fortunate to have seen one.

Acknowledgments

If stories were people, *The Skeleton Tree* would be Oliver Twist. Off to a bad start, it got a couple of whippings along the way, but turned out all right in the end. At least, I think it did. I'm very pleased with this story, and thankful to everyone who helped it along. Especially, I'd like to thank Kate Sullivan, senior editor at Delacorte Press. She's my Mr. Brownlow, the man who found an ailing Oliver and set him on the right path. But I'm grateful to many others as well: my agents, Danielle Egan-Miller and Joanna MacKenzie; Françoise Bui, my editor for many years; Kathleen Larkin of the Prince Rupert Library; Dr. Thomas Uhlig of Twin Cedars Veterinary Service; Beverly Horowitz and everyone else at Delacorte; my partner, Kristin Miller; my friends Bruce Wishart, Sheila Brooke, Darlene Mace and Joelle Anthony; my sister, Alysoun Wells; and everyone else who may have helped without knowing it, just by answering my many questions. Thank you, all of you.

About the Author

Iain Lawrence grew up moving all over Canada with his family. He worked in logging, fishing, and even as a forest-fire fighter before studying journalism in Vancouver and working at newspapers for ten years. He is the author of fifteen books for young readers and has received many accolades, including the Governor General's Award and the California Young Reader Medal. He lives in the Gulf Islands with his companion, Kristin, and their dog and cat. He invites you to visit him online at iainlawrence.com.